"Serena, y[...] anymore."

"Don't fool yourself, Brandon," she said seductively. "I know you better than you think. And I know me. I know what I want, what I deserve. I've always known."

Brandon watched her lift her arms behind her head and release the necklace she wore. The crafted gold dropped into the water with a gentle splash. Then she took off her bracelets, laying them by the fountain's edge.

"You deserve a man who can love you forever," Brandon continued, struggling against the overwhelming sexual tension surging between them. "Every woman deserves that."

Her laugh was bittersweet. "Yeah, we all do. But you know what? I'll settle for a man who will love me tonight. With all his soul." She stepped over the stone edge and into the pool, her fingers working on the knot on her skirt as the hem floated in the water.

"Serena," he groaned, aching to take her into his arms, into his life.

Her head tilted, ever so slightly, just enough for her eyes to catch a gleam of starlight and reflect her intentions. "Do I have to dare you, Brandon?"

Dear Reader,

I dare you.

Those three words tend to get any man's blood racing. But to a man named Chance, raised on the motto that a dare is a dare and a bet is a bet, that giving in is a sin of epic proportions, that phrase can spur a response that is certifiably wild.

And I like wild, especially in my heroes...and my heroines.

Now, I personally have three brothers. I know what it's like to mess with men who think they know what's best for them and everyone else. Like my brothers, Brandon Chance is certain he knows what he wants from life—and Serena Deveaux isn't it. Only, little does he guess that Serena is *just* the woman to turn his life upside down.

Chance brothers Kellan and T.J. won't escape the roller coaster of romance, either, not with authors Cheryl Anne Porter and Jill Shalvis writing their stories. Watch for #818 *Her Only Chance* and #822 *Chance Encounter*. And if you *dare* read any farther, let me know if you are pleased by the pay-off! Write to me at P.O. Box 270885, Tampa, FL 33688-0885, or choose my link at eHarlequin.com.

Happy reading,

Julie Elizabeth Leto

Books by Julie Elizabeth Leto

HARLEQUIN TEMPTATION
686—SEDUCING SULLIVAN
724—PRIVATE LESSONS
783—GOOD GIRLS DO!

PURE CHANCE
Julie Elizabeth Leto

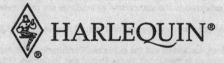

HARLEQUIN®

TORONTO • NEW YORK • LONDON
AMSTERDAM • PARIS • SYDNEY • HAMBURG
STOCKHOLM • ATHENS • TOKYO • MILAN • MADRID
PRAGUE • WARSAW • BUDAPEST • AUCKLAND

For the Leto brothers, Chris, Tim and Jason, who are just
as good-looking and adventurous as any romance hero
I've written—and even more fun! Thanks for being
proud, protective and supportive, for recognizing the
importance of family and for realizing that having a
tough, not-so-easy-to-intimidate sister isn't so bad in the
larger scheme of things. I love you guys!

ISBN 0-373-25914-X

PURE CHANCE

Copyright © 2001 by Julie Leto Klapka.

All rights reserved. Except for use in any review, the reproduction or
utilization of this work in whole or in part in any form by any electronic,
mechanical or other means, now known or hereafter invented, including
xerography, photocopying and recording, or in any information storage
or retrieval system, is forbidden without the written permission of the
publisher, Harlequin Enterprises Limited, 225 Duncan Mill Road,
Don Mills, Ontario, Canada M3B 3K9.

All characters in this book have no existence outside the imagination of
the author and have no relation whatsoever to anyone bearing the same
name or names. They are not even distantly inspired by any individual
known or unknown to the author, and all incidents are pure invention.

This edition published by arrangement with Harlequin Books S.A.

® and TM are trademarks of the publisher. Trademarks indicated with
® are registered in the United States Patent and Trademark Office, the
Canadian Trade Marks Office and in other countries.

Visit us at www.eHarlequin.com

Printed in U.S.A.

_____ Prologue _____

"WHAT DO YOU THINK you're doing?" Serena Deveaux demanded of her sister. Then she groaned as a wicked grin spread across Samantha's face like a lazy curve in the bayou—the kind with a hungry gator on the other side of a cypress, lying low until he could chomp off your leg for lunch. The devilish smile remained as Samantha drove past the corner of Dauphine and Esplanade, then double-parked while a woman with an armful of packages loaded her burgundy Mercedes.

"I'm waiting for that space," Sammie answered, drumming on the steering wheel with nervous energy. "You didn't think I was just going to drop you off? That wouldn't be neighborly."

"Neighborly?" Serena may have spent most of her childhood separated from her sister—she living with their mother in New Orleans and Sammie with their father in California—but she knew her sister didn't care two flips about being polite. "You're from Los Angeles. What do you know about neighborly?"

In the past, Serena wouldn't have teased her older sibling about her Hollywood lifestyle. Their relationship had been too strained by their parents' rancorous divorce to handle good-natured ribbing. But twenty-five years after the judge said, "Enough, already," and two months after Sammie abandoned her rental home in Pacific Palisades and her job as a movie stunt double to return to the French Quarter, they finally had a chance to be sisters again—teasing and all.

"If New Orleans is going to be my permanent home, I need to start thinking Southern. Listen to this." Sammie shoved her car into park, unbuckled her seat belt and turned to face her passenger. "Hey, Serena, where'y'at?"

Sammie's expertise with accents made her traditional Quarter greeting sound completely convincing. Serena couldn't help but laugh. Unfortunately, her mission this morning wasn't about laughter or teasing. It was about desperation and subterfuge and ridding herself of a dearly loved, but desperately unwanted, fiancé.

Drew Stuart, her unsolicited intended, had been her best friend since kindergarten. As she thought back over the years of scraped knees and quilted forts and stickball games in the street, she couldn't imagine how their friendship had taken such a dramatically wrong romantic turn. Just over a year ago, Drew started getting all mushy. Sending her potted plants with frilly ribbons. Buying her Valentine cards that didn't contain the usual rude joke or harmless insult. Talking about marriage. Marriage!

As if he didn't know that walking down the aisle with anyone was the last thing she'd ever do.

No thank you. She was only five when Devlin and Endora Deveaux split their family in half, separating Serena from her sister and her father, except for brief visits when the mood struck him. Heck, Drew barely survived the parting of his own parents just after high school. But one very determined bee had invaded Drew's marital bonnet and he was walking around with a ring in his pocket, waiting for Serena to lose her mind long enough for her to say yes to his proposal. She'd already said no, several times. He'd ignored her and booked the church. She'd tried refusing to speak to him until he came to his senses. He'd pouted until she relented, then chose their china pattern.

Well, enough was enough.

Serena wished her plan could be less complicated. Like the hand-painted tile hanging above her desk, Emerson's mantra of "Simplicity, simplicity, simplicity!" usually ruled her thinking. Once she discovered that transcendental philosophy in college, she'd clung to the idea in every aspect of her life. She worked for love, not money. Simple. She had an occasional lover, but no long-term boyfriends. Simple. She played hard and lived happy and planned to be single and unfettered for the rest of her life.

Apparently, not so simple.

"You'll be making crawfish étouffée and singing 'Iko, Iko,' any day now." Serena's compliment notched Sammie's smile from haughty to dazzling. She hated to tarnish the shine, but she really couldn't afford Sammie tagging along. "But could you think Southern tomorrow?"

Serena grabbed her thermos and a basket from the back seat, a homemade breakfast of café au lait and beignets. Suddenly, her offering seemed paltry for a man she was about to trick into becoming her accomplice in showing Drew the light. "I need to see Brandon alone."

"You? Alone with Brandon Chance?" Sammie's deeply set blue eyes widened. "As I recall, the last time you two tried that, things didn't turn out so well."

Serena squeezed her eyelids shut and winced. Had it really been fifteen years? She remembered the glittery streamers hanging from the gymnasium rafters. Balloons stamped with "Congratulations, Graduates" floating above the crowd. Zach Doucet spiking the punch his mother served from her best crystal bowl.

And Brandon Chance, her *other* best friend since the second grade, luring her into a dark corner and kissing her—a kiss that changed her forever—a kiss that mangled the one friendship that had always mattered most.

If she learned one thing from the incident, it was that friendships—like hers with Drew—were too precious to lose over romantic nonsense.

"That was a long time ago," Serena insisted. "I've practically forgotten all about it." If Sammie bought that lie, Serena would consider selling her prime real estate in the Bayou St. John.

"Brandon groped you, Serena. He was drunk and treated you like 'a Bourbon Street whore,' I believe you said…or perhaps I should pull out the letter you wrote to me shortly thereafter? I kept it, you know."

Serena shifted in the passenger seat, moving the warm basket of pastry from one side of her lap to the other. "You're a packrat, you know that?"

"So are you. Comes in handy sometimes."

"So do old friends. Brandon apologized. I accepted." *Too bad the damage had already been done.*

Sammie shook her head, bobbing her neat, blond ponytail. "But you haven't had a conversation with him since that happened, have you? He was your constant companion from age seven, more so than even Drew. You have a mountain of unresolved feelings for the guy, Serena. You'd better deal with that before you go waltzing into his office offering him...whatever you're offering."

Literally, she was offering him breakfast. Figuratively, she was offering way more than he'd ever accept—if not for the ace up her sleeve.

When Serena had heard that Brandon Chance had moved back to New Orleans and opened a bodyguard service, she finally saw a way to convince Drew that his one-sided romance would destroy their friendship—something she wasn't yet willing to let happen. Drew had been there graduation night. He'd seen what Brandon's fumbling, artless kisses and grabbing had done to her, the long-term price she'd paid. Drew had warned her countless times over the years that Brandon was the reason she refused to form long-term, intimate commitments. If she became involved with Brandon again, Drew would be the first one to warn her off.

He'd be the first to tell her that friends should never become lovers. The first to remind her of the pain and heartbreak of a one-sided attraction.

Hopefully, he'd finally see the light and drop his own fruitless pursuit before she had to cut out contact with him altogether.

All she had to do was hire Brandon as her bodyguard and then make the world—and Drew, in particular—believe that they were lovers. She didn't allow herself time to mourn the fact that fifteen years ago, he would have helped her just because she asked. Now, she had to resort to deception.

"I need Brandon's help with a professional matter," Serena said.

As the burgundy Mercedes finally vacated its spot,

color drained from Sammie's California tan. "Serena? Tell me this isn't about Brandon's new business. Has something happened to scare you?"

Scared? God, yes, she was terrified! Not of Drew and his proposal. She'd hurt him if she had to, sacrifice his friendship if he wouldn't back down. Marriage simply wasn't an option, though she'd try anything to avoid losing yet another cherished friend.

What scared her was the man in the office above. The one who'd taken her teenage crush and turned it into something heartbreaking and humiliating. The one who'd given her the sincerest of apologies, then abandoned her for fifteen years.

The one she had to face. Today. This morning. Now.

"Brandon's bodyguard business doesn't have anything to do with this."

Brandon Chance's retirement from the military had shocked more than a few Quarter residents who figured this particular native son to be an army lifer. The fact that he'd returned to open a personal-protection service incited gossips from the banks of Lake Pontchartrain to the Moonwalk. Even his Aunt Tillie, still best friends with Serena's mother, didn't know the nature of the career switch, though she lamented that he'd simply swapped one dangerous endeavor for another.

Serena didn't really care why he'd chosen to become a bodyguard. She just factored his new profession into her plan.

She had to remove marriage from Drew's agenda and restore the casual comfort of their friendship. She'd tried everything she could think of to do so without resorting to mind games, but buoyed by the support of everyone who knew them, her own mother included, Drew remained firm.

She had only one option left. Convince him she'd fallen in love with another man. But not just any other man.

Brandon Chance.

She couldn't remember now the precise moment she'd started fantasizing about Brandon, but the memory of making out with her pillow and pretending the soft, fluffy down was Brandon, stuck in her head. She was, what? Fourteen? With her double promotion into Brandon's class, she saw him every day—watched him flirt and tease girls who were obviously smitten with him—then he walked *her* home. Spent his free time with *her*. Yet even then, she'd known that initiating a romance would spell certain disaster.

She'd been right then. She was right now.

Unfortunately, Brandon's apology for his horrible behavior included a goodbye he obviously meant. He'd humiliated her with his clumsy kiss, but she'd paid him back by wounding more than just his pride that night with her muffled scream and resounding slap. She'd cursed their friendship, saying she wished they'd never met. And he'd made her wish come true. Since then, he refused to be more than a passing acquaintance.

If she wanted Brandon to help her, she'd have to hire him as her bodyguard. And to that end, she'd created the "Cliché Killer."

Her sister grabbed her hand. "Are you sure this is a good idea? You've been acting weird the past few days. I haven't been around you enough to know if that's unusual."

Serena chuckled and squeezed her sister's hand tightly. "Depends on who you ask."

Sammie rebuckled her seat belt and glanced into the rearview mirror, a sure sign she would give Serena the privacy she needed. "So I'm not supposed to worry? You want a private meeting with the boy—now the man—who broke your heart and I'm not supposed to be concerned?"

Serena opened the door and swung her legs out of the car, then tossed a sly glance over her shoulder. "Nope."

Sammie's mouth twisted with apparent disbelief. "Reassure me again *after* you've seen Brandon."

With that, Sammie rolled up the window and sped away. Serena watched until her sister's taillights whipped around the corner. Behind her, Brandon's office building loomed. Stepping toward the hewn stone stairs, she put down the thermos and basket and took a deep breath. Her heart slammed against her chest so violently, she felt sure she'd get the hiccups any minute. Or she'd pass out.

Fifteen years since he'd lured her to dance in a dark corner of the gym. Since she'd nearly fainted from overwhelming passion—a desire so incapacitating, her brain stopped working. For the briefest of moments, she'd thought he loved her. Like she loved him. That he wanted her. Like she so wanted him.

Then he'd kissed her. The alcohol on his breath had immediately quashed her raging hormones and made his motives clear. When his hand fumbled up her shirt, the last of her romantic notions deserted and her instincts kicked in. She'd slapped him. Then she'd run, straight to a chaperon who then dragged Brandon away by his collar.

All night long, she'd refused his phone calls, ignored the pebbles he'd flung at her window. She'd run like a coward. Away from the boy who'd befriended her on the playground and taught her about winning. From the teenager who'd driven her to her first nightclub and taught her how to dance the two-step.

From the young man who'd made her crazy with wanting.

The next morning, she'd accepted his apology. After a terse goodbye, he'd left only a few days later for a summer internship. He returned to New Orleans on an occasional holiday, and though they'd exchange small talk, Serena wasn't dense. Her fear and his screw-up had destroyed their relationship forever. He wouldn't help her salvage her friendship with Drew or take her job offer if she promised him all the money in her bank account. Nothing could undo the distance between them.

Nothing but the one thing Brandon couldn't resist...

1

LIKE TINY SOLDIERS snapping to attention, the hairs on the back of Brandon Chance's neck stood rigid and straight. The undeniably female form, visible but muted through the frosted-glass door between his bare reception area and his office, raised her arm to knock again. A jangle of bracelets accompanied her staccato rap, followed by a voice he'd know anywhere—a voice smooth like fine Kentucky bourbon, yet hotter than any Louisiana pepper sauce.

"Brandon? I know you're in there."

He watched the colors of bare flesh and bohemian clothes shift and writhe. She had her hands on her hips. She was probably curling down that bottom lip and deciding if he was worth the effort.

She knocked again.

He shook his head, wondering who he possibly could have pissed off so royally that they'd send Serena Deveaux to his office so early on his first day in business.

He considered blaming God, knowing He most definitely had a questionable sense of humor and a love for irony. But Brandon had been a relative saint over the past year and, so far as he knew, hadn't broken a single commandment. He'd watched his drinking. Given up cigarettes in the interest of healthy lungs. Hadn't even had a date that didn't end with a chaste kiss on the cheek—or worse, a businesslike handshake that made him wonder if he hadn't stayed in the army *way* too long.

But someone was getting a serious chuckle out of this morning's turn of events. Serena Deveaux, on the other side of his door, demanding entrance to his celibate life after years of deliberate separation.

"Brandon, open this door!"

"No Chances Protection is not yet open for business," he barked. "Call later and make an appointment."

Or better yet, don't call. Leave me alone. You're trouble, woman. The kind of trouble I'm going to avoid, even if it kills me.

True to the bold little girl he'd first met on the playground when she'd climbed too far up on the monkey bars to get down safely on her own, Serena grabbed the doorknob and turned. Luckily, he'd locked the door.

"If I didn't know better, I'd think you were *hiding* from me, Brandon."

He shoved out of his chair. *Chance men didn't hide.*

"I'm busy, Serena."

"Too busy for breakfast? A friendly peace offering?"

He didn't reply. In moments, he could see her frustration as clearly as if she stood right in front of him rather than on the other side of the door. At least from here, he didn't have to watch the way her wavy, caramel hair curved around her face and brushed her shoulders. Didn't have to contend with wide green eyes that could set his heart pounding with a single sidelong glance.

"The sooner you let me in, the sooner I state my business and leave. I have a friend who needs a bodyguard. Right away."

Brandon shook his head as he rounded the desk, wondering why he bothered delaying the inevitable. New Orleans, for all its various neighborhoods and outlying parishes, wasn't a big place—the French Quarter even smaller. Serena and her family—headed by her mother, Madame Endora, the foremost psychic in this booming colony of con men and swindlers— were relative fixtures in the Vieux Carre as much as the wrought-iron scrollwork and the Mardi Gras beads that dangled from them long after Fat Tuesday.

And since Serena now owned her own business in the heart of the Quarter, he accepted that he couldn't avoid her for long. Better to face her right here and now—in his office and on his terms. Surely he could trust himself to keep out of trouble long enough to hear about her friend.

He flicked the lock and pulled the door open, pasting on the stern expression he usually reserved for new recruits.

She countered with a grin that could boil sugarcane down to clear, hot syrup. Folding her arms, she caused her breasts to pout beneath a tank top tighter than a turn maneuver in enemy airspace. When she'd first knocked, only the hair on the base of his skull had sprung to attention. Now, other parts of his body followed suit, making him incredibly sorry he'd tucked his black T-shirt inside his equally dark jeans.

"You don't make it easy for a body to be friendly," she complained, her voice only half-annoyed as she turned to reclaim a basket and thermos from where she'd perched them on a tower of boxes near the door.

He returned to his desk and picked up an empty file folder. "I didn't come back to New Orleans to renew friendships."

At least, not ours.

He didn't need to share that sentiment aloud, and apparently, she didn't care one way or another. She shrugged and waved her hand in front of her as if she was clearing his negative karma from her path.

"You'd best rethink that strategy. Making a business work in this town is all about who you know." She dropped the basket in the center of his desk, unlatched the wicker and flipped back the top. A smell as sweet and light as pure heaven wafted past the dusty odor of half-unpacked boxes and freshly used gun oil.

"Beignets?" he asked, his tone entirely too wishful. "From Café du Monde?"

She grinned and shook her head. "Better. From Miss Lily's iron skillet. She told me to tell you she expects a proper visit from you before the week is out."

Brandon's mouth watered at the aroma of the hot French doughnuts. Mixed and fried by Serena's mother's lifelong cook and companion, the treats, their smell, instantly transported him back to the lazy days of his youth, back when he and Serena had been insep-arable friends. They'd stirred up and then avoided as much trouble as they could, running wild in the Quar-ter in the hot summers or caged in the halls of St. Simon's parochial school during the fall, winter and spring. She held the basket toward him, luring him into her personal space—space that just a minute ago had been *his* sanctuary. Serena invaded his office with the ease and confidence of a military leader staging an uncontested coup.

He just had to decide if he still possessed the ability to put up a potent resistance. He took a beignet from the lacy interior, then grabbed the whole basket just to show her who was boss.

Gesturing toward the thermos, he took a ravenous bite. "Is that café au lait?"

She twisted off the top with a similarly crooked grin and poured a generous helping into his army mug. "I added sugar before I left. You still drink it sweet, don't you?"

He answered by blowing on the coffee and taking a hearty swig. The bittersweet taste of coffee, chicory and milk heated his mouth, awakened his tongue and slid down his throat into a belly already blanketed by the doughnut. He could get used to such attention and culinary delight. In fact, he had an ironclad plan to find a wife as soon as possible who could whip up beignets and coffee that would beat even Miss Lily's in a taste test. Luckily for him, Serena's kitchen skills were limited to boiling water for tea.

"Tell me about your friend, the one who needs the bodyguard."

A tiny frown tilted her coral-tinted lips, then flitted away. "All business, huh?"

"That's why you're here, isn't it?"

She screwed the top back on the thermos and looked around his sparse office. He didn't have much to offer by way of seating. A metal folded chair sat in front of his secondhand desk and battered leather seat. A stack of boxes. A pile of books. She settled on the windowsill, her hands cushioning her thighs, her psychedelic wraparound skirt tousled by the breeze filtering in from outside.

"It's a fairly challenging case," she said.

"I'm listening."

"It may well be over your head, you being new and all."

Willing himself not to betray his emotions, Brandon leisurely leaned back in his chair and crossed his legs at the ankles. Inside, he raged with a simmering mix of anger, guilt and cynical suspicion—emotions only this woman could stir. Without much attention to subtlety, never her forte anyway, Serena was laying a trap. And since she knew him so incredibly well—fifteen years of relative estrangement notwithstanding—he wondered if he had the maneuvering power to steer clear of her snare.

Well, a Nightstalker pilot always had at least *one* option.

A bluff.

"You're probably right. I'm too new. You should find someone else."

He bit into a second beignet, careful not to breathe too hard unless he wanted a coating of powdered sugar all over his desk.

His easy retreat didn't phase her. She knew him better than to buy his sudden reluctance to take on a challenge beyond his ability. She dangled her sandals, watching her brightly painted toes as they swung above the baseboard.

"Nice try, Brandon."

"You don't know me anymore, Serena. Maybe I'm tired of danger and long-shot odds."

She snorted. "Maybe. But I'll *bet*—" she emphasized the word with just enough certitude to show him the direction of her strategy "—you won't be able to say no."

"Never make a bet you can't win, Serena. Didn't I teach you anything when we were kids?"

"Oh, yeah. You taught me a lot of things." For an instant, he thought he heard recrimination in her voice, but when he turned to look into her eyes—an error if ever there was one—he saw nothing but fiery challenge in her bottomless, gulf-green gaze. "Like the fact that you can't resist an honest wager, if the stakes are high enough. Are those darts?"

From her perch on the sill, she toed the brass case on the corner of his desk, drawing his gaze to the silky smoothness of her tanned leg and the glittering crystal dangling from her ankle bracelet.

He cleared his throat. "Yeah. So?"

"I bet you one bull's-eye, shot in our traditional manner, that you'll take this case."

He swallowed the last of his beignet and chased the doughy delectable down with half a cup of coffee.

"Do you think it's wise to gamble with your friend's safety?"

She leaned back against the window jamb, her hair catching the breeze and fluttering all too attractively around her cheeks. "I know what I'm doing. Do you?"

Brandon grumbled, certain he hadn't known what he was doing since he opened the door to let her inside. He'd spent fifteen years trying to keep Serena Deveaux out of his life. They were too alike—too reckless, too rash, too willing to throw caution to the wind and fly straight into disaster. He decided long ago to surround himself with people who would anchor him, keep him grounded and sane and out of trouble. For most of his adult life, that meant his army regiment, members of the elite Nightstalker squad—men who relished danger as much as he did, but had the discipline to pull back when ordered or when a battle couldn't be won.

Now that he was a civilian, Brandon had to find a new means to tether his wild ways. He certainly couldn't turn to his parents or brothers. Even Aunt Tillie had a devilish streak and a rap sheet. What he needed was a wife. A sensible, practical woman who would teach him the comforts and pleasures of home and hearth.

And though he hadn't done much by way of wife-shopping since his retirement or his return to New Orleans, he certainly planned to make it a priority soon. The sooner the better. But certainly not this morning. Serena Deveaux, beautiful and sexy and undeniably fun, was the most impractical, insensible woman he'd ever known. She would make his life interesting, definitely. But she'd also make his life hell if he gave her an opening.

On the other hand, if he played his darts right, maybe he'd turn the tables to his advantage, have a little fun before he got down and serious. He was a Chance, after all. Games and bets and high-risk ventures were his family's specialty. While he most definitely had his eye on a future with a stay-at-home wife, three kids and a huge mortgage, he'd long given up trying to *entirely* resist the thrilling lure of unknown outcomes.

He smoothed his hand beneath his collar, his scalp suddenly itchy and his shoulders tight. Of all the people in the world, Serena should have known better than to mess with him. A person didn't make a bet—

any bet—with a Chance unless they were completely prepared to lose.

Brandon eyed the polished brass case on his desk as he considered her offer. "I don't think this is a good idea."

Her sea-green eyes glittered with sunlight from the window, then crinkled deviously.

"A Chance backing down from an honest wager? There's an ancestor or two rolling around in their graves." She flattened her hands against the windowsill. "I can feel them."

Brandon shook his head, trying to remember if he'd ever met a woman who could pull off such swaggering self-confidence and still manage to look as fresh as a newly bloomed magnolia. Someone was definitely having a grand old laugh over this one. Here he was, hell-bent on starting a respectable life, and who sashays into his office but the playful, unpredictable sprite who'd taught him at a young age never to underestimate a woman.

"There are a lot of bodyguards in New Orleans, Serena. I'm sure you can hire someone else without resorting to games."

She shoved off the sill, clapping her petite, sandaled feet on his scuffed wood floor. She crossed her arms, adorned with swirling gold armbands that caressed her just above the elbows and a set of bracelets around one wrist, and jutted her slim hip to the left, her standard stalwart stance.

"That sounds weird coming from a man who's always treated life as a big competition. You don't like to lose, which should make you a perfect bodyguard." She picked up his appointment book, flipped the blank pages without comment, then set it aside. "Look, you don't want to work with me, but I want to hire you. You need the job, my friend has money to burn, and I *know* you can't resist the opportunity to beat me, even if it is just darts."

She opened the lid to the brass case, fingering the stiff blue-and-red feathers, raking her orange-tipped nails along the slim, shiny body of the dart, nearly pricking her finger on the razor-sharp tip. "I guess I'll just have to dare you."

He forced his gaze away from her and her haughty, naughty smile and judged the distance to his target. As much as he wondered why Serena insisted on spurring his competitive nature—and if he wasn't dreaming, his libido as well—instead of simply finding another agency, he wasn't about to ruin his perfect record by forfeit.

He'd just hung the dartboard this morning, directly across from his desk. He expected customers to be scarce until he drummed up interest in his protection agency. So he'd brought some toys along—the dartboard, two decks of cards and a handheld flight simulator—to ward off boredom while he worked on a business plan and made some calls. He had no idea Serena would drop in with a basketful of hot beignets, a thermos of café au lait and a challenge.

His grin widened with impending victory. "What are your terms?"

She matched his smile with a self-assured beam that was hers and hers alone. "Simple. When I win, you take the case. No arguments."

"And when I win?"

She shook her head as though the notion was as ridiculous as them ever rekindling the friendship they'd lost long ago. "Name your prize."

She stepped back and waved her hand as if she controlled the very air they breathed.

He ran a finger over the boxed darts, imagining he could feel the electric sizzle of her touch still crackling around the metal casing. "If I win, you're willing to do **wh**atever I ask you to?"

Serena snatched a steaming French pastry from the basket. "Last time I lost to you, I had to sing four verses of 'When The Saints Come Marching In' while dressed like Sister Mary Claire during the mayor's visit for Catholic Schools Week. Doesn't that prove I'm willing to do *anything?*"

Despite his every effort to remain aloof, he chuckled at the memory. The scene seemed as fresh as the breakfast she'd brought—Serena dressed in full black habit, singing off-key while Father Michael chased her around the cafeteria—all because Brandon's team beat hers in a Sunday game of corkball.

Unfortunately, dressing her in a nun's habit would seem like a crime against humanity today.

"I can be very imaginative," he warned her, closing his eyes against the images of Serena dressed in nothing but artfully woven feather boas, the kind she'd collected for years. "Still want to take the risk?"

She took a bite of the beignet, tearing a powdered, sugarcoated corner with straight white teeth, then licked the snowy remnants with a stiff, pink tongue. Hands on hips and eyes blazing, she locked her gaze with his.

"I triple-dog dare you."

His eyes widened. She'd skipped the double dare

and had gone straight to the ultimate challenge. The armor gauntlet tossed at his feet. The line drawn in the sand.

A feral growl vibrated in the back of his throat.

"Stand aside." He stretched his arms, hoping to send her scrambling back to give him some much-needed breathing room. He'd be damned if he missed this shot. He would *not* lose to Serena Deveaux, even if winning meant briefly letting her back into his life.

But she didn't succumb to intimidation easily. She never had. Gracefully, she twisted to avoid his stretch, but didn't budge an inch.

"Am I making you nervous?" She polished off the rest of the beignet in three ravenous bites, then licked the sugar dust from her ringed fingers. "I thought that secret military force you were in required nerves of steel."

She cleared a spot on the corner of his desk and slid her hip atop it—half sitting, half leaning so that her wraparound skirt flared enough to give him a second, longer glimpse of her smooth, tanned legs. The distinctive scents of magnolia and cinnamon wafted from her sun-kissed skin, scents he'd assumed until now had come from outside. The fragrance of the French Quarter surrounded her like her best feathered boa, all at once genteel and wanton. Lazy and sweet, but simmering with spice.

He cleared his throat and chose his dart.

"Stay where you are and watch how it's done."

Turning to face the window, he balanced the blue-feathered, silver-tipped dart over his left shoulder. He had to shoot backward—that was their traditional manner—but aiming placed her firmly in his peripheral vision. He closed his right eye. It didn't help. He took and held a long, deep breath, angling his elbow and forearm for optimum velocity and marksmanship. He cocked back, focused on the bright red dot at the center of the board and...waited.

He knew Serena. First, she'd try to distract him by coughing or sneezing.

She rewarded his suspicion with a mischievous grin.

Okay, maybe she'd graduated beyond uncontrollable noises to break his concentration.

So he waited for her last-minute question, the inevitable "Shouldn't you twist your shoulder a little lower?"

Thirty seconds passed. She pressed her lips together while she admired the condition of her fingernails.

Brandon found it hard to fathom, but perhaps Serena no longer stooped to juvenile antics.

Confident once again, he turned completely away from the target and prepared to shoot. That's when she combed her fingers through her wavy hair then let the caramel curls float in a breezy mass around her shoulders.

The dart found its home at the center of his unframed picture of Rush Limbaugh—a gag gift from his brother Kell, who insisted early retirement from the military would turn Brandon into an ultraconservative ditto-head. He winced and felt a phantom pinch in his groin in response to the throw. Too bad the photo wasn't just a head shot. Well, actually...

"Ha! I win." Serena's squeal and victory dance, a sweet little shimmy, increased the ghostly ache in his lower body to a very real pain.

"You haven't won yet." He should have guessed she

hadn't abandoned her modus operandi. She'd just changed her mode of distracting him to one he wouldn't anticipate. "You still have to shoot."

"All I have to do is make sure I don't emasculate Rush further," she taunted.

She licked her lips again, her grin crooked, but swallowed whatever indelicate comment invariably danced on the tip of her tongue—a very moist, very inviting tongue, Brandon thought as he watched her dampen her coral lips one last time while she picked a dart from the case on his desk.

The possibility of beating him polished her skin with a warm glow and rocked her hips in a slight but rhythmic swing left over from her victory dance. She could hardly contain her excitement. Brandon scowled, refusing to be drawn into her wicked web of mirth.

He stood his ground—though he did defer two steps to the right to allow her a fair angle—and tried not to think about what had changed so drastically about Serena Deveaux.

The smattering of freckles that once dotted her cheeks and nose had faded beneath the power of her sun-kissed skin. That night when he'd touched her in what must have been the sloppiest grope a teenage boy had ever attempted, her body had resembled the rigid grid of the French Quarter streets, all straight lines and sharp corners. Now, her arched cleavage, slim waist and rounded hips brought to mind the lazy curves of the Mississippi River and made him glad he'd come home.

Betting Serena would have ended up this gorgeous is one challenge he would have willingly lost.

She still brimmed with a love for life he'd never

known anyone to match. She still simmered with a fiercely competitive spirit she'd probably deny till the day she died. What he didn't know was how she, simply by filling out, could have him thinking about hot sweaty sex at ten o'clock in the morning. Especially after she'd left him cold all those years ago.

She winked at him before glancing briefly over her shoulder and firing the red-feathered dart with hardly a moment's preparation. The tiny thud of metal hitting crimson wood bloomed her Cheshire-cat grin.

2

BULL'S EYE.

She didn't even have the decency to make the shot look difficult.

"You've been practicing." He attempted a neutral observation of her improved skill, but still managed to sound surly. She rolled her eyes and retrieved the darts, crossing the room with the same flow of movement as her tie-dyed skirt.

He'd lost. At least now he'd find out the nature of his first assignment.

"I play a game or two when I eat at Rollo's," she explained. "He serves a mean oyster po'boy and reserves a board for Drew and me on Wednesdays." She leaned over to return the darts to the velvet-lined case, seemingly unaware of how the heady mix of spices clinging to her skin made him hunger for a lot more than a fried oyster sandwich.

He drained the rest of the thermos into his mug and downed the milk-and-chicory coffee in two large swallows. Aunt Tillie had mentioned the swirling rumors that Drew and Serena were planning to marry. For once, he'd doubted his aunt's usually impeccable sources. Serena had eschewed the institution of marriage her entire life, choosing her parents' high-profile divorce as a prime example that certain men and women had no business taking vows. She'd included herself in that list. He had no reason to think she'd changed her mind.

But apparently, she and Drew still hung out together. He shouldn't have been surprised. The three of them had spent more time together than some brothers and sisters he knew. The fact that the threesome had continued as a twosome after he left rankled more than it should have. Was he jealous? Please. He was just being nostalgic.

"Drew Stuart? You still hanging out with that geek?"

For the first time that morning, Serena's cocky grin faltered. "He's not a geek. He's just not a goon like you."

Brandon grabbed his gut and feigned an expression of pain. "That hurts."

She straightened her spine and impaled him with a no-nonsense glare that would have made his commanding officer proud. "Grow up, Brandon. I won the bet. I need a bodyguard and you're the man."

She punctuated her assertion with an orange-tipped fingernail, painted like a...sunset, he guessed, attempting to decipher the miniature scene upside down.

She glared at him until he met her stare with his.

"*You* need a bodyguard?"

"For my friend." She picked up his day planner again, attempting to hide her momentary fluster behind the faux-leather book. "Write in 'Serena's—seven o'clock.'"

"Your place? Serena, what are you trying to pull? If you're the one in danger..." *If you're the one in danger...what?* He would refuse to help her? He would let a fifteen-year-old wound to his male pride prevent him from protecting her from harm?

She hurriedly gathered the remnants of breakfast and tossed them in her basket. "Don't sound so hopeful, I'm just the 'contact.' Is that the word? It sounds so...intriguing." She wiggled her eyebrows and fingers, mocking the cloak-and-dagger element of his new job—the same rudimentary risk that drew him to the profession in the first place. After putting his life on the line for eleven years and sustaining himself on the rush, he'd chosen his new profession precisely because of the intrigue and danger.

Of course, not having been keen on taking orders during his former army life, he'd gone into business for himself.

He wondered if he would have made the same choice to start his new career in the French Quarter if he'd known Serena would be at the heart of his first job. She offered the last beignet to him, which he took, though he'd already eaten two. A deep-rooted craving stirred in his belly that had nothing to do with food. But since Serena was, well, Serena, he had no choice but to satiate himself with freshly fried and sugared dough. "So who's this *friend?* Criminal? Celebrity?"

She stuffed the thermos into the calico and lace-lined basket. "Just your average French Quarter business owner."

"Like you?"

She eyed him warily. "You know what I do?"

Aunt Tillie hadn't been stingy in her updates about Serena. Though he figured she would have used her multiple science degrees to discover a cure for the common cold or invent a vehicle that could travel at light speed, Serena operated some sort of beauty salon that catered to both the New Orleans elite and tourists alike.

"I heard you run a massage parlor." He couldn't resist teasing her. The instinct, as natural as blinking, imbued him with a vigor he hadn't felt in years.

"I have a *spa* on Toulouse Street." She pursed her lips, either cutting off a retort to his massage-parlor crack or fighting her urge to embellish her statement with more detail.

Brandon sat back in his squeaky new office chair, attempting to keep his assessment nonchalant. As long as he'd known her, Serena rarely answered direct questions without more minutiae. But replaying their short conversation this morning, he realized she'd been unusually tight-lipped.

Which meant, of course, that she was up to something.

Curiosity stirred. Serena Deveaux had never effectively told *him* an untruth. "A spa? What, like a gym?"

She shook her head and scooted his single folding chair nearer his desk. Turning the chair around, she sat sideways, one knee tucked beneath her, one leg jutted lazily to the right and her arms folded over the backrest. Except for the fact that she wasn't blond, she resembled an old black-and-white photo of Jean Harlow his grandfather had kept since the war. Her wide green eyes seemed weighted by her glorious fan of lashes. Her cheeks glowed with a natural color that bloomed as she spoke.

"No. Like a spa. Massages. Herbal wraps. Facials." She wiggled her fingers at him, making music with her bangle bracelets. "Nail art. I have a holistic dietician and massage therapist on staff and a signature line of natural teas and aromatherapy scents." Little by little, her intrinsic enthusiasm crept into her voice. He hadn't seen Serena in a long time, but he knew she wouldn't do anything every day unless she loved it.

"And you make money doing that?"

She rolled her eyes at him again, this time leaving them in a heavenward position for a long moment to express her exasperation.

"Let's just say I'm not starving."

He snickered. "That doesn't answer my question."

"Since when are you the fiscal patrol?"

"Since I left the service and have to pay for room, board and three squares. I've got a business to run." Adjusting to civilian life really wasn't as difficult as Brandon implied, but he did intend to make this business work on his own terms. "I can't waste my time watching one of your crazy pals burn incense unless I'm paid in advance, expenses included—bet or no bet."

When she slipped those blazing nails down the front of her V-necked tank, Brandon felt as if he'd just swallowed a desert sandstorm. His attention riveted to her breasts, she produced a small rectangle of green paper from beneath her purple top.

His gaze followed the treasure when she tossed it on his desk. From the visible corner, he recognized the check made out for fifteen hundred dollars. His fingers itched to caress the paper, still softened by the warmth of her skin.

"Will that hold you over for a few days?"

The ache in his groin, undoubtedly visible through the worn denim of his jeans, made him grateful he was sitting. He scooted closer to the desk, just in case. This woman was not the same Serena he used to play hide-and-seek with. Thinking about finding her in a dark, secluded space rushed a torrent of moisture into his mouth—until he remembered the last time he'd lured her into a dark, secluded space.

Guilt nagged at the edge of his consciousness. He hadn't exactly given her much warning, coming on to her on what should have been the best night of her life. Friends didn't paw each other behind the bleachers. But friends also didn't slap each other and run off to hide.

"I'll manage," he answered. He pocketed the check quickly, before his brain could fully register the effects of the moistened paper on his libido.

She stood and stared at him for a moment, the slight indentation in her cheek telling him she was biting the inside of her mouth. Like gnawing her nails, her habit was an old one and, obviously, one she hadn't over-come. He decided she wasn't lying to him. But she was holding back details—details that might make him de-cide not to honor their bet. Of course, he was a Chance, one of the last descendants of a long, infamous line of gamblers, speculators and die-hard risk-takers. He'd honor the terms or die trying. That was in the family creed.

And damn it, Serena knew that long before she'd come knocking on his door.

"Good. My house, tonight, at seven." She wrote her address on the back side of a New Orleans Events flyer he'd brought up from his mailbox. "We'll have dinner and discuss your...assignment."

"I need to know more before then."

She pondered his request a moment. "The assignment will probably last two weeks. Yeah, that ought to do it." The last comment, clearly meant to be thought, not spoken, engaged his internal radar.

"Serena, what aren't you telling me?"

She stood and straightened her skirt. "We'll talk tonight."

"Why not here and now? What are you trying to pull?"

"Pull? Me? Gosh, Brandon, don't you remember what a bad conniver I am?" She masked her face with a fake glaze of innocence and backed toward the door. "Remember that time I tried to trick you into eating those super-hot chilies?"

"You ended up eating them yourself. And drinking an entire gallon of milk out of my fridge." The memory, once again, made him chuckle. "I couldn't have my Wheaties the next morning."

His physical condition back to a relatively normal state, Brandon stood, sensing a crack of weakness in the confident air she'd surrounded herself with all morning. He edged around his desk, his gaze locked with hers.

"You survived," she reminded him. "I had heartburn for a week." She felt around behind her for the doorknob.

He took a few more steps in her direction. An underlying panic flashed in her eyes. He was making her uncomfortable. Good. Since she'd come into his office, he'd experienced a lack of balance and control that was entirely her fault. "You deserved it. It was a dirty trick you tried to pull."

"I had a good reason."

"As I recall, you always have a good reason."

She turned to open the door. She glanced over her shoulder, her eyes bright and her smile sincere. "That's one of the things you can count on with me, Brandon. I have good reasons for the stuff I do."

She slipped out before he had a chance to reply. *Good reasons.* Like when they were nine and she roped him into playing Prince Charming in her children's-theater production by promising he could use a real sword and kiss Renée Perkee on the lips. Or when she volunteered him to teach the entire faculty of St. Simon's High School how to play craps for Casino Night, a talent your average eleventh-grader wasn't supposed to have. Or the night he was so far out of line, he should have slapped some sense into himself.

Serena Deveaux, for all her strange ideas, then and now, never failed to make his life interesting, unpredictable. Much like his missions with the Nightstalkers. Toying with the eyeglass case on the corner of his desk, he wondered if the corrective lenses inside would have given him the edge to beat Serena at darts. He'd become adept at compensating for his failing eyesight, until his fuzzy vision nearly cost him his life and the lives of his crewmen. So he'd retired. And after eleven years in the service, he could use a little temporary fun. He could definitely use the fifteen hundred dollars.

Serena knew anybody and everybody worth knowing in the city and beyond, thanks in part to being the child of New Orleans' foremost psychic medium and a famed Hollywood director. She had more contacts than the security system at the Pentagon and could be just the ticket to launching his business with a bang.

That she'd transformed into a sexy minx made the prospect all the more challenging. And a Chance *never* backed down from a challenge.

AT THE BOTTOM of the stairs, Serena slid down and put her head between her knees, lifting her eyes once to smile at the sour-faced glare from some woman with horrendous taste in hats. But even the purple chapeau with silver ostrich plumes couldn't distract Serena for long. Had she owned smelling salts, she would have taken a big whiff right about now—anything to undo the unexpected effects of being alone with Brandon Chance.

She settled for a vial of lavender oil she wore around her neck. Dabbing two drops in the palm of her hand, she took a deep whiff. She could barely breathe. Panic remained twisted around her lungs.

Panic and something she didn't want to acknowledge—raw, lustful desire.

Brandon, like all the Chance men—younger brothers, Kellan and T.J., included—had always been a looker, but until sometime in her junior year, she'd never allowed herself to think of him as anything more than a surrogate older brother. Little by little, her feelings for him became what she'd thought was a harmless crush—a teenage attraction that wouldn't amount to anything more than a pleasant memory. That's why she'd reacted as she had all those years ago. He didn't have any business touching her like that, kissing her like that, making her feel things a girl not yet seventeen shouldn't feel.

The remnants of her reactions rushed back. When he'd lured her into that darkened corner of the gym,

her heart had beat more furiously than a summer rain-
storm on a tin roof. Then, he'd grabbed her, kissed her,
sloppy and drunk and fumbling with her clothes, until
she could do nothing but fight to get away. His apology the next day had been hard to hear, and even
harder to accept. But she had, unwilling to lose her best
friend over a stupid mistake.

Yet she'd lost him anyway. And no matter the sizzling attraction and sexual awareness that had as-
saulted her in his office, she couldn't allow chemistry
to cloud her thinking. Her "affair" with Brandon
would be a fake one, for the sole purpose of forcing
Drew to see that his marriage quest was ruining their
relationship.

She ran her hands through her hair, realizing that
with any other man than Brandon, she would not ignore the messages her body was sending. She had
never denied herself the pleasures of romance, the in-
timacies of adult interaction. But Brandon was everything she wasn't, even if they'd once had so much in
common. He'd always been somewhat cynical. Inherently competitive. Driven. More inclined to conquer
the world than make peace with it. As anxious to discover puzzles and contradictions as she was to avoid
them and just enjoy the moment.

Simplicity, simplic...

Emerson's mantra died before she reached the third
repetition. Simplicity and Brandon Chance didn't co-
exist. The man was complication personified.

Yet, here she was, nearly thirty, not inexperienced,
and the man had her heart doing back flips. Not to
mention her liquid, hot reaction to his thick black hair,
piercing gray eyes and broad, square shoulders.

She was a real sucker for big shoulders.

Maybe this was all a very bad idea.

Lord, Brandon Chance was one gorgeous hunk of man.

No.

She stood up, took a deep, cleansing breath, fluffed her hair and willed her heart to stop doing gymnastics. She'd protected herself from his misguided magnetism on graduation night; she'd do it again.

Reinvigorated by her resolve, she stepped into the sunlight and down the stone steps. Sniffing her palm again, Serena headed toward Esplanade Avenue on her way back to the spa. She needed something stronger than aromatic oil to restore her balance— she'd mix up a cup of her special brew, maybe schedule a massage.

The side street was quiet. Cars lined the stone curb, and at least one idled nearby. With a quick glance left and right, Serena stepped in front of a parked sedan and started across the street. She was halfway to the other side when a black car peeled off the curbside and barreled straight toward her.

3

BEFORE SHE COULD react, a body, hard and lean, half tackled, half carried her onto safe ground. She landed in a circular bed of ivy with Brandon Chance and his gorgeous mass of male muscle firmly atop her. The roar of the speeding car died away, leaving only the sound of her heartbeat and panted breaths—intimately commingled with his—to break the sudden silence.

That, and Brandon's muttered curse. "Does the word *ditz* mean anything to you?"

Wind absent from her lungs, Serena coughed into the green leafy vine and threw her elbows back until Brandon grunted and shifted to the left, allowing her room to steal some air. But not much. His shoulders and chest and stomach and hips pressed against her like a living brick wall, hard and hot and heavy, in a way that wasn't entirely unpleasant. Not unpleasant at all.

"No, but *oaf* is suddenly crystal clear." She struggled beneath him, shoving against him with her backside without thinking of the consequences. Sexual awareness jolted through her and rooted her to the spot. His erection pressed against her bottom sent a surge of pure lust to every erogenous zone in her body—a few she hadn't realized existed until right now in the grass. The yin and yang of basic need—his hard to her soft, his male to her female—grabbed her at the core and held her captive.

She willed herself to speak. "I know you hate to lose, but isn't this a bit extreme?"

He rolled over, grunting when his back met the chiseled stones separating the ivy from the grass. She rediscovered her ability to breathe.

"In case you didn't notice, I just saved your life." His tone demanded her undying gratitude.

Men.

"Delusions of grandeur," she mumbled, pulling herself onto her knees. "I would have made it out of the way on my own."

A cool spring breeze drifting up her thigh brought her attention to the state of her skirt. Treating him to a view of her panties furthered the indignity of crouching on all fours in a pile of foliage. She yanked her skirt down and growled at him all in the same breath.

That arrested his attention. His gaze immediately caught her dash for modesty, and she didn't miss the cloud of disappointment that darkened his eyes from silver to thundercloud gray. "And what if you didn't?"

"The car would have swerved."

Except that it hadn't. The fact obviously occurred to Brandon at precisely the same moment. His gaze turned from skeptical to accusatory.

She moved to stand on her own, but he grabbed her elbow and pulled her up with him instead. With a tiny bounce, she landed inches from him, her nose even with the base of his throat.

"*You* need the bodyguard, not some friend."

Serena glanced back at the road, quiet now that the car was long gone. She just hadn't been looking where she was going. The driver probably wasn't paying attention. And she'd been distracted by the unwanted and unexpected return of her adolescent lust for Brandon. She'd looked both ways, but hadn't checked for cars pulling out of curb spaces. No one was *really* trying to hurt her.

Unfortunately, she couldn't tell Brandon that just yet.

"I'm fine," she insisted.

"That's not an answer, that's an evasion. Are you in danger?"

She slapped the clinging ivy leaves from her elbows and knees, then plucked wayward twigs from her hair. "No. I mean, no, I don't think so." She shook her head, realizing this incident could help her cause. She needed him to believe she was in danger, just not until tonight when she'd had time to prepare. "Not at this precise moment," she amended.

"Not at this precise moment." He repeated her words exactly as any disbelieving, retired military-commander-turned-bodyguard would. Understated annoyance clung to his clipped tone. Then he bit his tongue and growled much as she had earlier, though the guttural grumble rumbling from his throat made him a rottweiler to her Chihuahua.

He tugged her by the elbow out from under the tree, and quickly surveyed the area, holding her close. His cologne—musky without a hint of spice or sweetness to offset the overwhelming masculine scent—nearly kept her from noticing he was now in bodyguard mode. Except she didn't want him on the job. Not now. She had work to do this morning. A lunch date with Drew she simply couldn't cancel, not when she planned to set the wheels of progress in motion after dessert. Brandon could start tonight. After work. After dinner.

After I have time to squelch my raging hormones.

She tried to wrench her elbow free, but quickly learned the power of his grip. "What are you doing?"

"You paid for three days' worth of protection. Consider the meter running."

"I don't want the meter to run." He glanced at his watch as if noting the time. She tugged at the nylon band. "Turn it off! I'm fine. The car was a fluke."

He twisted his wrist from her grasp, yet kept her firmly in his. "But you did hire me for yourself, didn't you?"

She refused to answer. Couldn't answer. The feel of his hands on her—of his body on hers—overrode her ability to contain a situation that had already gotten out of her control.

"Have you received threats before today? Before that car tried to mow you down?"

"That car didn't try to mow me. It was an accident." She struggled against his grip again, huffing when her actions proved fruitless. She'd have to try reason, which as far as she could remember never worked with Brandon once he made up his mind about something. "I wasn't paying attention. I must have stepped into the street without looking. It happens all the time. Well, not to me, but to other people."

Brandon half listened to her attempt at rational logic while he scanned the street for any sign of danger. Determining the immediate area secure now that the dark-colored, older-model Chevy Corvette Stingray was long gone, Brandon turned his attention squarely to Serena. She wasn't biting the inside of her mouth, and her eyes, liquid and lucid and green as the gulf, fairly begged him to believe her.

She could be right. He'd been so intent on catching her to return her frilly basket, he hadn't noticed the Corvette, either, until he'd stepped between parked cars. His crack observation skills allowed him to recognize the make and model. He might have caught the license plate if he didn't hate wearing his glasses so much.

"Maybe the car was an accident, but that doesn't explain why you went to such interesting lengths to hire me." He released her arm, wincing inwardly when he noticed the ring of red his fingers left on her skin. "'Fess up."

Stalling, she made a production of ensuring the straightness of her clothes. "'A deal is a deal and a bet is a bet.' Isn't that your family motto?"

He couldn't contain a crooked grin. Serena remembered the damnedest things from their childhood. "Something like that. So you didn't think I'd help you unless I put Chance honor on the line. Why not?"

She shrugged, then proceeded to pluck leaf bits and mulch from his shirt. "Do I have to remind you?"

Her fingers were quick and nimble, her eyes entirely focused on him and his chest, reminding him why they were no longer friends. He took a step back and divested himself of foliage remains with two large sweeps of his hand. "That was a long time ago, Serena. I got over you."

She glanced aside, silently chagrined. "Of course you did."

But had he? Really? He couldn't deny that Serena

didn't fit into his carefully crafted plans for his future, but he also couldn't ignore that since she'd walked into his office, he'd never been so aware of a woman in his life. That cognizance acted like a current of electricity, imbuing him with an energy he hadn't felt in months— if ever. Except for that one infamous instant years ago, Brandon had always been better, smarter, stronger because of Serena.

He wouldn't let her down now, even if it meant spending every minute of his free time in a cold shower until he got to the bottom of her problem. "What kind of threats have you been receiving?"

She hesitated and Brandon immediately saw her intention to weave a tale. With a hard glance, he convinced her otherwise. She breathed a reluctant sigh.

"Just notes and stuff," she admitted.

"What kinds of notes? Do you still have them?"

"I threw them away."

"No, you didn't. You're not that dumb."

"I threw the first one away."

"That's natural. But the others?"

"Printed on a computer. Inkjet. Standard paper in a plain business envelope. They were slipped into my newspaper after delivery. None of my neighbors saw a thing. The threats are impossible to trace."

"I'll be the judge of that. Where are they?"

"At home."

"Let's go."

"I have a staff meeting and a client appointment in an hour. I can't be later than I already am."

Brandon closed his eyes to keep her from seeing them roll upward. He had no right to belittle what she did. Despite her wacky ways, Serena had the brain of a rocket scientist. She could have joined NASA or gone to MIT and graduated with honors had she wanted to. But if she preferred brewing weeds and mixing mud masks for rich socialites, who the hell was he to judge?

"We'll go to the spa first and then head to your house. It will give me a chance to check security at your work."

"I don't want you scaring my clients. I worked very hard to create a clean, relaxing atmosphere."

Brandon could practically hear the wind chimes and koto music and smell the smoking incense. Not his kind of hangout, even for a brief stay. Places like that made him jumpy, as if the atmosphere could melt through the carefully crafted walls he'd built around his private thoughts. To avoid the place, he would have challenged her to a rematch at the dartboard...if not for one important detail.

Serena might really be in danger. Though she insisted the near miss with the car wasn't intentional, the fact remained that she'd hired him as her bodyguard. Serena was a do-it-yourself kind of woman. She wouldn't ask for help—especially from him—unless circumstances left her absolutely no other choice. He'd seen her get herself into and out of trouble more times than a petite little brainiac like Madame Deveaux's oldest daughter should have. Between "Cyclone" Serena and "Dippity" Drew, her eternal sidekick, Brandon's childhood had never been boring.

Why she'd come to him was baffling, but he couldn't contain the slight but warm puffing of his chest. He'd always been her ace in the hole. He wouldn't let her down.

Not this time.

"No one will know I'm there," he insisted. "Where's your car?"

"I don't have one. I caught a ride here with my sister. I planned to walk back."

He fished his car keys out of his pocket and pressed them into her hand. "Mine's the black Jeep parked on the corner. Start it up while I lock my office."

Her palm and fingers, soft and warm and smelling of something floral and sweet, felt small in his hand, but strong. Powerful, even. Yet hers was a power he knew and needed to avoid.

"I'd prefer if you came by later tonight." Her suggestion, clearly a last-ditch effort and accompanied by a tilted grin, cured his momentary lapse. He dropped her hand. Keeping her in his grasp this time had nothing to do with protecting her or ensuring her safety...just plain old sexual attraction.

"Go start the Jeep, and lock the doors. I won't be two minutes."

Serena accepted his decision with her usual aplomb, twirling toward his parking place with grace. He watched her walk to the car, every sultry step down the entire block. When she disengaged the alarm and slid into the driver's seat, he remembered he had something to do.

Back in his office, he loaded his gun, slid into his shoulder holster, pulled on a light sports coat and engaged the answering machine. Before locking the door, he slid his glasses onto his nose and stuffed the case in his pocket as he headed toward his car. Knowing Serena as well as he did, he'd have his work cut out for him figuring out who'd sent the threats. Notwithstanding the few times he'd wanted to wring her neck himself, he couldn't imagine anyone wanting to hurt Serena.

His investigative training was still fresh. His mind quickly but methodically ran through the procedures he'd learned from the intelligence officers he'd worked with, as well as from his training at his former commander's protection agency in Miami. Serena would be a reluctant client, the hardest type to protect. If he had any brains, he'd ditch her at her office and make a run for it to save his fledgling career.

But he wouldn't. A Chance didn't retreat.

He grabbed the car latch, silently cursing the damn family-honor code. *A deal is a deal and a bet is a bet.* Several generations of gamblers and risk-takers had imbued Brandon and his brothers with the inability to back down from a challenge—especially when wild cards were thrown in, making the outcome that much more unpredictable.

And Serena Deveaux was the wildest card he knew.

She unlocked the door when he knocked on the window. In an off-pitch voice, she sang along with Heart's "Never" playing on a classic-rock radio station, while drumming her palms on the steering wheel.

"Get in." She squeezed the words in between two lines of the verse.

Leaning against the open door, he watched her bob to the bass beat, wondering how the heck he was going to survive the next hour, much less the three days to two weeks she planned to employ him.

"No way. You ride shotgun."

Turning up the volume before she exited the vehicle, she slid out of the seat and bopped to the beat all the way around the back of the Jeep. Brandon quickly glanced around, but the surrounding block was clear. He'd talk to her about being less conspicuous later.

They'd be safe once they reached the heart of the Quarter. Serena was weird, but would blend in with the oddballs he'd seen hanging around Jackson Square. Seems Serena, once only privately goofy, had overcome her reserve on all fronts.

Lucky him.

He didn't have the heart to lower the radio volume until a commercial for potato chips provided a break to the music. He'd stopped at a light on the corner of Dauphine and Toulouse and watched the tourists crossing one block up at Bourbon. The Quarter hadn't changed all that much since he left after high school, except the tourists were more plentiful and enjoyed their hurricanes and daiquiris a little earlier in the day. Serena didn't seem to notice the crowd, though she did roll down the window to shout to a hansom cabdriver and his mule, both by name and with separate salutations.

She directed him up Toulouse, then jumped out of the car before he had time to pull in to a coveted parking space near the corner at Royal.

"I'm late. Meet me inside."

She disappeared into the storefront of Serena's Spa and Scents without incident, so Brandon parked and cased the block on foot. He'd seen no sign of the Corvette during their drive or as he walked the distance from the antiques shop on the corner to Decatur and back. Maybe she was right. Maybe the car incident had nothing to do with the threats she'd received. Of course, he'd never know until she filled him in, something she seemed oddly reluctant to do.

Brandon tucked his glasses back in their case and

yanked open the shiny black, glass-paned door into Serena's shop. A soft jingle brought him to the attention of the college-age guy manning the reception desk.

"Welcome to Serena's. You Brandon?"

Brandon bit down his impulse to tell the kid to stand straighter and get a haircut. "Me Brandon."

"Cool. Serena said to fix you a cup of tea and show you round." His voice was an odd mix of California surfer-dude and high-country Creole. "Chamomile or green?"

"Excuse me?"

"Tea. Don't drink it, right? I didn't either till Serena recruited me, man. Can't live without the stuff now. Clears the brain." He mimicked the cleansing effect with a waving sort of gesture, then reached out to shake Brandon's hand. "I'm David."

Brandon resisted the temptation to show him the grip of a man who started his morning with strong Cajun coffee not girly tea, but the boy was young, no more than twenty. No longer responsible for breaking in new recruits, Brandon cut him some slack.

"Work here long?" he asked. Might as well start his investigation with her employees. Even without knowing the nature of the threats, he could store any information away for later.

"Over a year. Since I started Loyola. Serena schedules work around my classes, and she, like, guilts me into studying when things are slow. She's ultra, you know?"

He'd never heard the expression, but understood the meaning implicitly. *Ultra.* Beyond the ordinary.

A perfect description.

"Yeah, I know." Brandon declined the tea and proceeded to look around. As he left the waiting area through a drape of crystal beads, he relegated David to a low slot on his so-far empty list of suspects. The boy's admiration for his boss was fairly obvious. He had no observable reason to threaten her.

In the main spa area, shafts of prismed sunlight broke through the beveled skylights, some stained blue or green, and dappled the thick white carpets and shiny marble floors with the colors of sky and sea. Mirrored walls on three sides reflected the sylvan artistry of the garden outside, fully visible through floor-length windows and a double set of French doors.

Unlike many of the gardens tucked behind the homes and businesses in the Quarter, this one had been totally refurbished, scrubbed clean and polished to a New Age glow. The lawn—short, cropped and green enough to make the caretakers of Augusta similarly colored with envy—sported walkways of smooth granite and trimmed topiaries. The privacy wall was tiled with massive squares of marble. The central fountain, white as genuine alabaster, trickled drops of clear water over an abstract shape Brandon immediately found erotic. He stepped closer to the French doors, trying to determine what exactly in the fountain's shape made him think about sex, when Serena's lilting purr beckoned from the threshold to her office, a small room in the far-left corner, partially hidden behind a mirrored door.

"Soothing, isn't it?"

Soothing wasn't the word he'd choose. For the fountain or its owner. She'd tidied up since their nosedive into the ivy. Her hair shined as if recently brushed, the curls softer, the natural gold highlights brighter. Her lips glistened like the water slithering over the polished, curving shapes of the fountain—stirring images of tongues and flesh and wet, wet heat.

"Captivating."

"You think?" She moved toward him, her walk rhythmic, her voice soft, as if they discussed some intimacy rather than outdoor art. "I had it commissioned last year. It's an interpretive piece. The artist claimed it would intensify the feelings and emotions foremost in the viewer's mind."

That explained the eroticism. Since this morning, he'd had little on his mind other than sex and Serena.

"My clients seem to believe it works."

He dug his hands deep into the pockets of his jeans. "And these clients...what? Ask you to conjure up a gris-gris to make their troubles disappear?"

His comment came out more belittling than he intended, but from the way she stuck her tongue out at him, she hadn't taken the jab to heart.

"I run a spa, not a voodoo shop. That's Endora's realm. And I'm not telling you anything more about what I do if you're going to make fun. You can just do your security check and wait for me in the lobby."

Feeling appropriately chastised, Brandon considered her suggestion, then decided he genuinely needed to know more about her business—for the sake of his investigation, of course. A little "bad mojo," as his aunt called it, could make a client very angry. And since Serena's mother, Endora, was still the reigning queen of New Orleans mysticism, Brandon suspected Serena's tearoom and massage parlor dealt with more than ginseng blends and aromatic oils.

"I didn't mean to make fun. I just never thought you

actually believed the mumbo jumbo your mother makes her living with."

"I don't." She folded her arms as if to cross them, but forced them to her sides with a huff. "Not entirely." Taking a deep breath, she closed her eyes, paused, then reopened them and spoke with a serenity she was wildly trying to cling to. "My methods are scientific to the greatest extent they can be. Herbs and teas have the power to positively affect different parts of the body. A lot of your run-of-the-mill psychological or emotional problems can be eased this way. They help a person cope better."

"You're not a licensed holistic doctor."

"No, but I have one on staff. My specialty is teas and aromatherapy." She crossed her arms over her chest, abandoning her battle with defensiveness. "And I do hold a degree in chemistry, in case you forgot."

And one in physics. And one in accounting. Serena bit down hard on her tongue, causing a stabbing sensation that ran straight to the center of her indignation. And anger. And more than a little annoyance. All negative emotions she tried daily to purge from her life. She hated justifying herself to anyone as much as she abhorred throwing around her degrees to gain credibility. It wasn't her style.

She entered the garden, slowly inviting the warmth of the spring sun to bathe away the negative karma Brandon brought with him. Without sunglasses, she squinted into the late-morning sky. The sun, currently angled into the spa's garden, lit the tiny specks of glass imbedded in the granite walkway into flames of cool fire.

She loved the garden this time of day, before the

rush of lunchtime clients. She glanced at her watch, noting that she didn't have much time today before she had to meet Drew at the Court of Two Sisters for a meal with a potential client of Drew's and his wife. She'd have to cancel. Either that or bring Brandon with her. No time like the present to set her plan in motion, right?

"I'd like David to run me a list of your clients," Brandon said. With his shoulder propped against the doorjamb, he crossed one black sneaker over the other in a pose of perfect manhood-at-ease. Perfect, *sexy* manhood-at-ease. Brandon's presence in close proximity to the sculpture she'd found erotic since the artist delivered it nearly threw her into carnal overload.

"What for?" She sat on the fountain's ledge and dredged her hand through the water, sparkling sapphire and emerald as the sun above met the small mosaics below the surface. The sculpture behind her was set so the moving water caressed the curves and then dripped into the turquoise pool from smooth points of stone…that suddenly looked like nipples. When Brandon pushed off the doorjamb and joined her, her body temperature rose at least two degrees.

"Suspects. I won't know what I'm looking for until I see the threatening letters, but I should get the ball rolling. I offer a full-service plan—investigation *and* protection." For an instant, he spared the sculpture a quick glance, then sat with his back to the fountain and stretched his long, lean legs across the narrow walkway. He either wasn't affected by the marble's sensual curves, or she just didn't inspire the same arousing thoughts that he did for her.

She fought the urge to splash him. She fought the

urge to splash herself. She'd asked him here. Heck, she'd triple-dog dared him right into the center of her personal life. She had no right to complain, no matter how dizzy he made her.

"Suspects, huh?" Exposing her clients to his merry wild-goose chase hadn't been her intention, but Brandon couldn't make a case out of something that didn't really exist. She'd gone to great lengths to make sure her faux threats could not be traced to anyone in particular—especially her. "Tell David what you want. He's a whiz on the computer. Consolidated my entire database over Christmas break."

"David seems to like you a lot. Maybe a little too much?"

She dramatized her smirk with a grunting sigh. He wasn't serious, was he? "He's a kid. Like a little brother."

"To you, maybe, but what about to him?"

Well aware of the dangers of unrequited lust, Serena shook her head. "I'm one hundred percent certain that David's feelings for me are completely platonic. Leave him alone. Unlike you, he wouldn't threaten a flea, even to help the dog."

"Unlike *me?*" Hostility deepened the furrow in his forehead.

"I didn't mean it that way." Serena nearly reached for his hand, but fought the urge. Touching him would be a mistake of epic proportions. "Just don't waste your time or your suspicions on David. He and I have been alone a million times. If he wanted to hurt me or come on to me, he would have."

She glanced at her watch, then stood and smoothed away the imaginary wrinkles in her skirt. "My client will be here soon. Can you make yourself scarce for a while?"

He shook his head, his smile fixed. "You didn't pay me to be scarce. You'd better get used to me, Serena. Until I find out who threatened you, you bought yourself a shadow."

4

SERENA SAT, hands firmly beneath her thighs, trying desperately to keep her attention on Drew's clients, and her fingernails out of her mouth. She could feel the heated weight of Brandon's gaze along the side of her neck. As far as she could tell, he hadn't taken his eyes off her. Not once. Not to order his meal at the table hidden by the lighted ficus to her left. Not to eat. Especially not when Drew draped his arm across the back of Serena's chair. The possessive gesture suddenly made her feel guilty, as if she was doing something horrid, like perpetuating a lie—which she was, on so many different levels her head spun.

Just yesterday, the idea of resorting to half truths and a few bald-faced lies had seemed a small price to pay in pursuit of the greater good. Now, Serena wasn't so sure. Brandon wasn't the average, easily distractable male. Her flirting this morning might have helped her achieve an easier victory with darts, but she couldn't count on feminine wiles now that Brandon was on the job and in such close proximity. In fact, unless she wanted to invite some serious trouble, she had to figure out a way fast to rein in her instinctive responses to his potent masculinity.

If not for the heavenly scents wafting from her barely touched plate, she'd probably still smell that musky essence of his. She still strongly recalled the warmth of his body engulfing hers when he'd tackled her to the ground. The memory of him pressed hard and firm against her made her want to wriggle right out of her skin...and right into his.

"Serena, are you all right?" Drew cupped her shoulder and she nearly jumped out of her chair, bobbling her water goblet so that four pairs of hands reached out to catch it.

She uprighted it first, then dabbled a few wayward drops with her napkin.

"What? Oh! Sorry. I'm not hungry today. Tough morning."

Drew's clear blue gaze followed hers to the lighted plant. He leaned back so his line of vision could bypass the ficus tree to what was drawing Serena's attention on the other side. Silently, Serena prepared an explanation for Brandon's presence. But when Drew turned around, his boyish grin was a mixture of patience and relief.

Serena bent forward around Drew and peeked past the tree herself.

Brandon was gone.

She glanced apologetically at the Smithfields, the New York couple sitting across from them, probably wondering if they should invest in Drew's company when his supposed girlfriend was more interested in decorative foliage than his pitch.

"Would you like a mimosa? Or a Mai Tai?" Mrs. Smithfield held up her drink and shook it, as if the swirling pink liquid could chase away any and all ills.

Serena might have believed a double-bourbon straight up could do the trick, but not today.

"No, thank you." She replaced her napkin on her

lap, fiddling with the angle across her skirt. "I don't drink on Tuesdays." She picked up her ice water and took a deep swig. It was sound reasoning not to drink on Tuesdays, though she regretted her vow today. Designed to keep her out of trouble during Mardi Gras, dry Tuesdays were suddenly a risk to her mental health.

Obviously, Mrs. Smithfield didn't grasp her logic. "Why not Tuesdays? Is it your religion?"

Drew capped his hand on her shoulder again, a little roughly this time, to stop her from answering. "Just a quirk. Serena's got a million of them. It's why I love her."

Except that he didn't love her. He just didn't realize it. Just as he wouldn't admit that he'd silenced her to keep her from beginning the inevitable debate on the topic of religion. If he had the gumption, Drew could make himself a millionaire by writing a book on how to effectively avoid conflict and still get what you want.

"That's me." She smiled dopily. "Quirky ol' Serena."

The relief on Drew's face sparked her ire nearly as much as the unexpected return of her attraction to Brandon Chance. Men! Nothing but trouble since that day in the Garden of Eden.

"Excuse me, Miss Deveaux?" A green-jacketed waiter interrupted with a slight bow. "You have an urgent message at the bar."

"Probably something at the spa. Mother must be late for the afternoon readings again. Excuse me, please." She laid her napkin across her seat, grabbed her bag and wove through the heavy lunch crowd of business executives and tourists, leaving Drew to explain her cryptic comment to his guests.

Just as she expected, she found Brandon leaning impatiently against the bar to the right of the maître d's stand, his arms crossed leisurely over that impressive chest of his, his sports jacket hugging his incredible shoulders with a delectable snugness.

"If you wanted to talk to me, you could have come by the table." Her fervent whisper was nearly lost under the merriment of the crowd. "Why be so secretive? It's just Drew."

He eyed her narrowly and she used every ounce of her grit not to look away. Before they entered the restaurant, he'd explained why his job required he blend into the shadows at this point. While his course of action didn't bode well for her plan to convince Drew that she and Brandon were involved again, he didn't know that—yet.

"I'm trying to be inconspicuous, remember?"

Serena sniffed and gave him a very conspicuous, very complete appraisal of his new attire. Dressed in black jeans, a black polo shirt and matching sports coat, he looked like the devil on a mission of seduction—a mission he might succeed at if she didn't prevail over her hormones.

"I hate to break this to you, Brandon, but you can't do inconspicuous. It's invisible or nothing for a guy like you."

"Is that a compliment? Or a come-on?" He shifted his weight, releasing his arms and adjusting the angle of his shoulders and hips so she suddenly felt as if he'd closed the space between them, though he'd barely moved.

She swallowed the measly amount of moisture in her mouth and decided her best defense was selective hearing and a quick change of subject. "Is something wrong? Or do you have to leave?" she added hopefully, crossing her fingers in full view, until she noticed her hands shaking and tucked the gesture behind her back. She'd been away from him for over an hour, and yet even at a distance, he'd invaded her personal space like bead-seekers on Fat Tuesday. Now, pressed closer by the crowd in the bar, his scent and warmth enveloped her once more, along with that infuriating cocky grin.

"I want to get to work," he answered. "I'm not learning anything about your stalker by listening to Dippity Drew spout Internet projections and cost estimates."

Dippity Drew. She hadn't heard that in a heck of a long time. "Name calling? Haven't you outgrown anything?"

Other than your clothes? And me?

"I'm kidding. The Drew-boy wouldn't take me so seriously."

She frowned, knowing he was right—and worse, knowing there was a time when she didn't take him so seriously either. Drew always laughed at Brandon's jokes, no matter how raw they sounded to her. Boys operated on a different level sometimes, a lower level.

"Well, the 'Drew-boy' doesn't know you're here."

"Brandon? Brandon Chance?"

Her indignation caught in her throat like a wad of caramel-coated popcorn. And she hated popcorn.

"Drew-boy!" Brandon reached past Serena and grabbed Drew's outstretched hand, pumping with an enthusiasm that engaged Serena's dishonesty radar. "Didn't know you were here."

And from the look on his face, Drew's radar clicked on as well. "Serena's having lunch with me and some clients," he explained. "Didn't she tell you?"

"He knew." Resignation tinged her retort. "He's teasing."

Drew smiled boyishly and swept aside a constantly unruly lock of his blond hair, reminding Serena how she missed the old days when being Drew's friend meant sharing her new pack of baseball cards or telling Sister Frances Patrick that *she* shot the spitball at the blackboard to keep him out of trouble.

Sometimes, being an adult sucked.

"Haven't changed much in that department," Drew answered, still smiling, still unaware of how Brandon's return was about to disrupt his life. "Heard you'd retired from the service. Opened a detective agency or something?"

Brandon didn't elaborate, but engaged Drew in harmless talk about computers, Drew's family and the Saints' most recent losing season. Serena tried to find her soft place, a comfortable mental zone of blooming gardenia and trickling brooks and no men in any proximity, especially not these two, acting like long-lost brothers and dashing her plan to hell. Then Brandon grabbed her fingers, jolting her back into the restaurant with an electric flash.

"Then Serena brought me breakfast this morning and I finally felt at home again. I have to thank you one more time." He looked at her as if no one else in the world existed. He was flirting, shamelessly. Unfortunately for her ego, Serena knew his attention was only meant to annoy. And though his teasing aided her plan to convince Drew that she and Brandon were destined to reunite, she couldn't help rolling her eyes, knowing only Brandon could see her reaction.

"So you *did* know Serena was here." Drew's lightning-quick glance at her hand, entwined with Brandon's, formed a marble-size pit in the back of her throat.

The seed had been planted—her plan was now in motion. *No turning back now.*

"That's why I came." Brandon's smile tilted with such mischief, he reminded Serena of the time he tied her training bra to the flagpole on the back of his bike. If she didn't tread carefully, she'd end up just as humiliated as that day on the playground.

Drew wasn't a fool. He knew her very, very well. Knew Brandon well and the long history of their fitfeen-year-old acrimony. That's why she'd chosen Brandon, she reminded herself, no matter how much risk she took with her own heart. *No risk, no gain. No risk, no gain.* The chant wasn't exactly Emerson, but it had seen her through more than a few tight spots.

"Brandon, Drew and I are having lunch with—" She started to put an end to his charade when he winked, effectively cutting her off.

"I really have to talk to you, Serena. Privately."

His words could have meant a thousand things if not for the sultry rasp in his voice. In a tone meant for candlelit tables in a back corner booth, he established an intimacy between them more effective than anything she could have concocted.

The question was, Why? Still, she played her part by matching his seductive whisper.

"I really can't. Drew's clients..." She shrugged, implying she'd rather not return to the table.

Drew didn't miss the hint, but he continued genially. "If I handed them a pen and a contract, they'd sign right now. Talk to Brandon."

He squeezed Serena's shoulder before he stepped away, then turned back and kissed her on the cheek. Pressing his lips against her skin hard, he startled her with the intensity. Usually, she and Drew parted with a brief sweep of mouth to skin, barely touching, the contact not as important as the gesture.

This time, her friend attempted to brand her, and the desperation in it nearly broke her heart.

"I'll call you next week," Drew said to Brandon. "We'll have a beer after work?"

When Brandon agreed, Drew disappeared into the dining room without a backward glance.

Though he had no way of knowing her plan, Brandon's intimate capture of her hand and rumpled-sheets whisper had helped her cause. Drew *never* engaged in public shows of affection. Because normally, she'd deck him if he did. Brandon's presence evoked exactly the response she'd hoped for, but she'd arouse Brandon's suspicions if she didn't act at least a little irked. He didn't, after all, know that she wanted him to play the part of her lover.

Did he?

"What was that?" she asked.

"I want to see those threats."

"That's not what I'm talking about." She raised her hand to his eye level, so he could clearly see his fingers still clutching hers.

His pupils grew larger, darkening his eyes to the

same pewter hue of her grandmother's antique musket. The effect was just as deadly. When he increased the pressure from his callused fingers, Serena swallowed deeply, then rooted her feet into an even-keeled stance—so if he did something unexpected like kiss her hand, she wouldn't faint right there on the polished stone floor.

He drew her arm closer. She stepped nearer. His gaze lingered on her trembling hands, then he met her breathless stare with another wink. "It *is* a sunset."

"Sunset?"

"On your nails. The manicure you probably paid too much for." He dropped her hand with disinterest.

She may have paid five dollars a finger, but she'd risk destroying them for one good swipe across his smug face. Lord, this man provoked her violent nature without hardly trying!

"You were flirting. Was that just to annoy Drew or were you trying to make him jealous?"

"I'm just your bodyguard, Serena..." Grabbing her elbow, he wound them through a party of six toward the door. The hallway between the restaurant and the street was wide and dark, with smooth stone walls on either side that made the short space cavernous and private all at the same time. Once the doors to the restaurant shut, he swung her back against the stones and blocked her body with his. "Not your lover. Why should Drew be jealous?"

She blinked as her eyes adjusted to the sudden darkness, but she could do nothing to make her body adapt to having him so close physically—and mentally. He was on to her. Somehow, in typical Chance fashion, he'd figured out her scam. Either that or he was fishing.

Time to turn the tables with the most powerful weapon in her arsenal—the truth.

"He'd be jealous because he knows how I felt about you—once."

"What? That you hated me for treating you like a cheap slut on graduation night? I apologized for that, Serena. I meant every word."

She saw the self-recrimination in his face, deeper and darker than it had been fifteen years ago when he'd sobered up and then bit out an apology. His words then had undoubtedly soothed his conscience more than they had her hurt feelings. He was a guy, after all. She hadn't expected him to understand the depth of his betrayal. And she'd never had the opportunity to explain.

Until today.

"Brandon, I only hated you for about fifteen minutes. You broke my heart that night, you know? Not the way a lover does. After a while, girls learn to chalk that up to experience. I lost a friend that night. That's worse. *That* stays with you."

He nodded, then hung his head for an instant before glancing back up at her with eyes of pure silver, cleared of the gray storm clouds that shadowed them all morning. When he licked his lips, her heart slammed against her ribs so hard, she felt certain she'd shaken the stone she leaned against. His face inched toward hers, mouth slightly open, wet and warm and inviting.

"Yeah," he agreed. "That does stay with you."

She flattened her palms on the cold, jagged wall, grasping for a handhold to keep her from falling—back into the web of his mystique, back into the desire she thought she'd beat so very long ago.

Too late.

Her lips parted to suggest they leave, to insist they take this somewhere private, but she caught the words with a gasp when the door from the street swung wide, allowing a bright gleam of outdoor light to stream into the dusky hallway. He pushed off the wall.

The air around her instantly changed, even before three tourists walked between them to go inside. Like a curtain tugged partly aside, the hurt from the past had eased, but the attraction most definitely had not. It just jumped up a notch from instinctual to inevitable.

Brandon dug his hands into his pockets, his back flush with the opposite wall—as far away from her as he could manage in the enclosed space. "I acted with my hormones and not my head that night, Serena. That was wrong."

She grinned, knowing from personal experience how hard apologies were for Brandon. "Your head wasn't exactly clear either, if I recall." She laughed lightly, hoping to abate the tension a bit more.

His smile revealed her success. "No, it wasn't."

Then the humor disappeared. His mouth tightened. His eyes squinted, as if his facial expression alone could convince her of his new resolve. "But I'm thinking clearly now, Serena. I shouldn't have flirted with you back there. And just now…"

"Just now, what?"

Serena had to know. If the attraction between them was not one-sided as she'd first believed, she had some serious decisions to make. Like whether or not to go on with her scheme at great risk to her heart. Or whether or not she should explore her desire for Brandon—to find out if it was just a physical attraction born from what-ifs, or a simple chemical reaction that could be sated then forgotten.

"You almost kissed me, Brandon. Why?"

He shook his head, grabbed her by the elbow, roughly this time, and pulled her toward the door. "Because you make me crazy, you know that? Let's get out of here. We have a stalker to find."

Serena contained the thrilling wave of triumph bubbling inside her. *She made him crazy.* From anyone else, the words might have offended her. But from Brandon, the admission was inherently self-satisfying. Maybe he hadn't written her off so easily when he'd left New Orleans. Maybe his kiss-and-grope fifteen years ago wasn't just a drunken, nonsensical mistake. Maybe, just maybe, he'd wanted her. Like she'd wanted him.

Like she still wanted him, she finally admitted.

She followed him into the sunlight, digging her sunglasses out of her bag. This was a turn of events she hadn't expected. The stakes in her little game just rose to high-roller level, but Serena decided she wouldn't cash out just yet. The jackpot was too tempting, the prize too alluring, to ignore. She might not be the one with Chance for a last name, but she certainly enjoyed risks and payoffs as much as he did.

And very soon, she would show him how much.

ONLY SERENA COULD make unlocking a door erotic. She bent over to peer directly into the antique keyhole, then shimmied her bottom while she worked the skinny key into the lock. She'd twisted her hair into a loose knot atop her head secured with a chopstick she'd found in her purse. Soft caramel curls kissed the back of her neck, in precisely the spot Brandon would choose to kiss if he was ever insane enough to come on to her again.

He had no idea what had come over him at the restaurant. Maybe it was his lifelong rivalry with Drew for Serena's attention, maybe the quaint atmosphere of old-fashioned romance at the Court of Two Sisters. Maybe he'd just been without a bedmate for way too long.

And maybe the same unalterable attraction that had led him to grope her that night in the high-school gym had returned, with a vengeance.

He shifted to the left, shoving the cooler she'd asked him to pick up from the spa onto the scrollwork railing of her front steps. Dredging up old, better-forgotten memories wasn't going to help him with his first order of business: finding out who was threatening her life.

"I'll upgrade the locks on your doors tomorrow morning. If someone was chasing or following you, you wouldn't have much luck getting inside quickly and safely."

She stood up and brushed aside her bangs, her forehead gleaming with moisture.

"This is the original doorknob. And key." A long red tassel twisted around her wrist as she held the key aloft. "Do you know how many people have handled this? No one's lost it in one hundred years. That has to mean something good."

"It'll mean something better if your place is secure. I'm changing the locks first thing tomorrow."

"There's no—"

She cut off her argument by swinging around and

manipulating the metal mechanism until he finally heard a loud click. Brandon had the distinct impression the lock wasn't the only thing Serena was manipulating. More than once today, she'd insisted she wasn't in any danger, despite that she had several threatening letters and had shelled out fifteen hundred dollars as a retainer for his services. She was up to something. And he had no doubt he'd soon be finding out exactly what.

She used her shoulder to shove the solid oak door open. Tossing her large, hand-woven bag onto an antique secretary in the front hall, she waved him inside.

The walls were pink. Not little-girl pink, Brandon decided as he strolled over a genuine wool carpet much like the ones he'd bought for his mother in Istanbul, but a berry shade that reminded him of lipstick. A Tiffany lamp worked with the stained-glass sidelights to bathe the front entrance in a muted rainbow of jewel tones. Antique portraits, some framed in gilded squares or fruitwood ovals, covered the entire wall. The faces were young, old, male, female, aristocratic and common—all hung together in a haphazard collection of portraits.

"Your relatives?"

Serena had already made it to the back of the house. Situated in a double-shotgun style, the house allowed her a quick beeline from the foyer through the parlor into the kitchen. Unlatching the back door, she turned to see what he was talking about.

"You like my gallery?"

"A motley bunch."

"That's what I like about them. I collect portraits

from antique shops and estate sales. Some belonged to clients."

"You don't know any of these people?"

"My great-aunt Aggie is the second in the third row."

"The rest are strangers?"

"They welcome me home every day, so I don't really think of them that way."

Brandon shook his head, wondering if Serena really knew what a stranger was. Even when they were young, her mother let her wander the Quarter with little-to-no supervision. She made friends with the shop owners, surrey drivers and street performers, who looked out for her as if she were their own. She sought out the tourists, trading directions for descriptions of their hometowns or tales of their travels. She was an irrepressible mix of charm and sociability and intelligence. How could anyone want to hurt her?

Then again, he'd hurt her once, but not intentionally. When he'd made his sloppy attempt at seduction, he'd wanted nothing more than to please her—pleasure her in ways a boy of seventeen had no skill in doing. What resulted was her shock, her humiliation, her anger. Then she'd forgiven him the next day without berating or badgering. And he'd repaid her by staying away.

At the time, his motives had been honorable. He and Serena, since they'd met as children, brought out the devil in each other. They tempted fate and pushed the rules, creating a childhood of fun and frolic that he'd never forget or regret. But as an adult, he saw that her influence on him wouldn't help him attain his goals, or vice versa. They each needed someone to balance and ease their adventurous natures.

That's why the teasing, the flirting wouldn't happen again. Beyond protecting her, beyond keeping her safe, he refused to relive the disasters of the past. And short of welshing on his bet, he'd do everything in his power to maintain a safe distance between this woman and his heart.

If such a goal was possible—even for a Chance.

When she opened the back door, a flying mass of four-legged fur bounded in from the screen porch. Wet-tongued and panting, the long-haired mutt of massive size and questionable parentage tackled Serena to the floor. Brandon tensed at the threat, then relaxed. Of course she had a dog. She probably had an entire kennel in the backyard.

After scanning the street once more for curious eyes, he closed the front door and set down the cooler. He watched her roughhouse with the dog, it yelping and her squealing, and decided she was as wondrous now as she was when they were kids—even more so. She twisted his hormones into a badge-winning knot with her heady blend of childlike enthusiasm and subtle seductiveness. One afternoon with her, and it was oh-so-easy to pretend that they'd never been apart.

As Brandon stepped out of the foyer, the dog immediately stopped playing and stood alert. Brandon halted. The dog might act like a puppy, but his jaws looked as powerful as the row of teeth he'd suddenly started to bare.

"Maurice, out!" Serena commanded.

With a canine "harrumph," Maurice closed his mouth and sat, a body full of long, straight hair flowing up, then settling onto the floor like a carpet with a dog underneath.

"Brandon, meet Maurice. Maurice, this is Brandon. He's a friend." She called Brandon over with a wave of her hand. He approached warily, his left hand extended.

Obediently, Maurice sniffed Brandon's hand, then his leg, then panted a doglike smile.

"He likes you," she concluded.

"What is he?"

"Part sheepdog, that I know."

"You rescued him from the pound, no doubt."

"Nope. He showed up at the spa one day. I gave him a bath, a bowl of vegetarian chili, a doggie massage and a home. We've been best pals ever since." She fluffed his ears while she talked, and the dog leaned his full weight against her as his back paw tapped the floor with growing speed. He nearly knocked her over again until she pushed him aside.

"Big baby. Find the cat, Maurice." He cocked his head at her request, paused a moment as if to translate English into dog-speak and then tore off toward the front bedroom.

Brandon glanced around the kitchen. Done in wood only slightly lighter than the mahogany and cherry in the foyer, the space had been brightened with flowered wallpaper on a field of white and a forest of houseplants hanging from copper baskets and perched atop expertly carved cabinets. Lace covered her kitchen table and hung around the large windows that looked onto a whitewashed back porch. From front to back, this house had a woman's touch—more like a woman's punch—on each and every surface. He never would have expected such domesticity from her. "Nice place."

"Thanks. Miss Lily decorated it for me."

That explained the hominess.

"You live by yourself?"

Funny, he hadn't thought to ask until he found himself alone with her.

"Always have."

"The dog's good for security."

"He's a marshmallow."

"Doesn't matter. A big dog is a big dog. Do you keep his bowl in plain sight?"

"It's on the porch. He stays there most of the day and can go in the yard through a doggie door."

"A doggie door? They make them that big?" He considered the security risk of a man-size flap entrance until he realized what it advertised. "I guess someone would have to be suicidal to try to come in that way. Are there any other entrances to the house other than the front and back doors?"

She shook her head.

"Good. That'll make securing this place easier."

"Is all that necessary?" she protested, then added, "I don't want to change the house much. It's on the historical register."

"Didn't the notes all come to the house?"

"Yeah."

"Then it's necessary. Can I see them?"

Twisting her mouth in a wary expression, Serena gestured toward the parlor. He followed her into a room brimming with antiques. Floor-to-ceiling windows allowed muted, natural light—but more importantly, showed him that the alleys on either side of the house were securely gated. Her home faced a quiet street in a residential corner of the Quarter. Either Serena or a previous owner had torn down the inner walls of the original two-family home to create additional space inside, but the close proximity to the houses next door would make an unnoticed stranger highly unlikely.

"How long have you known the neighbors?"

She sifted through the contents of a wooden box she'd slid from a bookshelf, digging until she found a folded sheet of plain white paper, just as she had described. "Since we were kids. They all know my mother, too. In fact, every house on this block has at least one family member who's a satisfied, return customer of Madame Endora's."

He unfolded the paper, miffed that exploring that angle would probably end up fruitless.

"'Life is short?' That's it? You consider that a threat?"

"Read the back."

Brandon flipped the paper over. This time, the words weren't typed in a plain, computer-generated font like the main message on the inside. They were done with elaborate color graphics—small, block letters dripping with blood. "'For you.'"

He nodded and refolded the paper. "When did you get this?"

She tapped her toes and studied the carpet, shrugging rapidly as if she wanted to dance—or leave. "Last Monday."

Again, she answered his question without detail. Either the threats scared her more than she would willingly admit or she wasn't being entirely truthful. Both scenarios made his job more difficult.

"And you found it..."

"Tucked in with my newspaper."

"Did you question your delivery guy?"

"Armando? Yeah. He didn't know anything about it. He folds and throws the papers himself."

"What time does Armando deliver?"

"Around six."

"What time do you bring it in?"

"Probably seven. After walking Maurice."

"Where are the others?"

Not once during the entire exchange did she look up from the antique casket brimming with colorful cards, flimsy pink and yellow receipts, assorted news articles and envelopes stuffed with licenses, certificates and warranties. Not exactly the most congruous place to store threats on her life. Yet Serena had always been a living, breathing lesson in irreconcilable differences. Just look at the two of them.

She scratched the back of her neck, then kneaded the muscles before diving back into the wooden box. She found two more notes, both similarly folded, on exactly the same paper. He read the threats, starting with the typed phrase on the inside and following with the bloody punch line.

"'Time flies...when you die.' 'All's well...that ends in hell.'"

She shut the box and put it back on the shelf. "I guess he likes clichés."

"The Cliché Killer. How perfect for the media."

Serena rubbed her hands up and down her arms. "He hasn't killed anyone."

"You don't know that. You also don't know that this psycho is a man. You don't know anything about this creep at all. Serena, this is serious. Are you sure you've told me everything? Shown me everything?"

"I hired you as a bodyguard, not a detective."

"Some agencies, like mine, specialize in both. I can't do a very good job of protecting you if I don't know the nature of the threat. And unless you want to pay my fee indefinitely, I should try to find out who's sending these, don't you think?"

She nodded, then wordlessly slipped back to the kitchen to unpack the cooler, avoiding his gaze from start to finish. He tapped down his growing frustration with a deep breath. He couldn't remember Serena ever avoiding trouble, much less ignoring it completely. Why would she start now, with her life on the line?

Tossing the threats back into the casket, he crossed to the kitchen and watched her prepare dinner. At first, her movements were jerky and quick, but slowly, the tension eased from her shoulders. She stopped twice, her back to him, and paused just to breathe. He couldn't tear his gaze away.

Right then, Brandon knew, he was in big, big trouble.

She slipped the chopstick from her loose twist of hair and the soft curls spilled onto her shoulders. Combing nimble fingers through the waves of sunset brown, she sighed. The sound, barely audible yet brimming with a lethal mix of fear and frustration, tugged at a piece of his heart he'd tamped down a long time ago. He still cared about her. Still wanted her. Still craved the one prize horrible timing and horrendous manners had denied him.

His keen desire tugged him, urged him nearer. When she began massaging her temples, he longed to slip into the space behind her, his hips pressed to hers, his fingers tangled into her hair as he commandeered the circular motions with his own hands. Unlike this morning in his office, Serena wasn't flirting to distract him—and yet he couldn't keep his mind focused on figuring out the cryptic threats or enhancing security or anything except touching her again. What a sap he was! Here he was lusting like a green cadet after basic training and she didn't know he was there.

Or did she? Brandon grinned, then cleared his throat and scowled with all the severity he could muster.

"I don't think you should stay here alone tonight."

Serena winced when she should have rejoiced. Just as she'd schemed, Brandon was about to become her roommate. With him under her roof, she'd quickly convince Drew that she and Brandon were mad, passionate lovers. She didn't doubt that Drew would then rush to warn her about her infatuation with Brandon in the past—how mistaking friendship with romance had set her up for tremendous heartbreak—and she'd throw that illustration right back at him and force him to face the truth.

"If you really think that's necessary," she conceded, too overwhelmed to argue, even for the sake of appearances. Brandon was about to stay the night, in her house. He'd shower in her bathroom, sleep just a few feet away in the spare room. Would she sleep at all, knowing he was near enough to touch?

"Absolutely necessary," he declared. "So, should you call Drew, or should I?"

5

"CALL DREW?" She banished the squeak from her voice by clearing her throat while she wiped her hands on a clean paper towel. She scooped up the oversized bowl she'd just filled with Asian chicken salad, and with every ounce of calm nonchalance in her burgeoning supply, carried their dinner to the table. "I don't need Drew's permission for you to stay the night."

He paused before he spoke, causing Serena's spine to vibrate with anxiety. Just how much did he know about her and Drew and her "situation?" Likely more than she bargained for.

"You sure about that?" he asked.

One look into Brandon's suddenly unreadable gray eyes told Serena to proceed with caution. A tinge of suspicion, coupled with a teasing lilt that had none of the playfulness or humor she'd once grown accustomed to, made her believe that Brandon wouldn't see the brilliance of her plan too easily—especially since she'd gone so far as to show him the fake notes.

"Are you afraid to stay with me? That's gotta be hard on the bodyguard business."

His scowl motivated her to grab a knife and begin slicing bread at the kitchen sink. She tried to concentrate on cutting the crusty loaf in equal, even portions—anything to fend off the haunting feeling that she'd just kicked a hornet's nest with a sharp-toed shoe.

"That line doesn't work anymore, Serena."

He pushed off from the doorjamb and approached. Serena felt each and every noiseless step as if the space between them stretched with an invisible, elastic force. Taut yet pliant. Supple and subtle and sizzling with an undercurrent of volatile energy. He stopped not two inches away from her. His words accompanied a breeze of hot air that singed the curls at her nape.

"You're hiding something," he whispered, his fingers barely touching the small of her back. "We may not have seen each other in a long time, but you've always been an open book to me." He slid his hand from her back to the curve between her shoulder and neck. Fingering her hair, he teased her earlobes with the intimate strokes of his hand and heated breath. "What aren't you telling me?"

Serena slowly placed her serrated knife back on the cutting board. Her hands shook. Attempting to cut even crusty bread could be dangerous. Though at this very moment, she could think of nothing more perilous than standing in her kitchen with a man who exuded sexual energy with the same unstoppable force as the Mississippi River during a flood. Sheer stupidity and fear had allowed her to fend off that attraction once.

What could possibly save her now?

"I've told you everything you need to know," she insisted, hoping a degree of honesty would stall him.

He snatched a chunky slice of bread and took a hearty bite. "And I don't need to know that you and Drew are engaged?"

Anger fueled by familiar annoyance gave her the strength to push away from him to retrieve a breadbasket from the hutch. "Who told you that?"

His eyebrows raised at the tastiness of the whole-grain bread, and he popped the rest into his mouth, chewed and swallowed. "My aunt scorched more than a few fiber optics delivering that news. None of those rings you wear are diamond solitaires, but I figured you to pick something less...conventional."

Serena looked at her hands before shoving them onto her hips. "I'm not wearing a diamond solitaire because I'm not getting married. To anyone. Ever."

He didn't react in the least to her claim. He'd heard it before, years ago, but with enough repetition that she felt certain he hadn't forgotten. Still, she would have felt better if he reacted a little. A smile, maybe? Relief?

"Have you told Drew?" he asked.

Serena gnawed the inside of her mouth, putting aside her own ridiculous fantasies to deal with the here and now. Here she had the perfect opportunity to come clean. To be honest. To seek his help without lies and half truths and open-to-interpretation excuses. "Yes. Several times, as a matter of fact."

"And...?"

The expression he wore gave her absolutely no clue as to how her admission had affected him. In fact, she was certain her marital status meant nothing to him at all. She shouldn't be surprised. She definitely shouldn't feel disappointed.

But she did.

She risked approaching him again long enough to fill the basket and place it in the center of the table. Breaking through a decade and a half of Brandon's indifference toward her wasn't going to be easy, but Serena knew she was going to have to try. And not because of her kooky plan. Because she wanted him to care, darn it! The way he used to.

"Drew doesn't believe me," she explained. "He thinks I'm just being stubborn."

"Stubborn? You?"

"Coyness doesn't become you, Brandon." She grabbed plates and glasses and set them on the frilly place mats she kept on the table. Usually alone, she rarely ate without a newspaper or book to distract her. What she wouldn't do for a nice thick copy of *War and Peace* right about now. "He's known me as long as you have. I have a certain reputation for being true to my convictions."

"You mean for being pigheaded."

"You're impossible, you know that?"

"I've heard. From you, as I recall. On more than one occasion just today, as a matter of fact."

She turned to the refrigerator and yanked a tall amber bottle from the wine rack inside, remembered today was still Tuesday and cursed before sliding the Chardonnay back in place. She rummaged instead for a can of soda, grateful Samantha had left one of her caffeine-loaded, artificial-coloring-and-flavoring favorites behind the remnants of the cheesecake they'd shared last week. She preferred alcohol at times like these, but would settle for sugar.

Grabbing the largest goblet in her eclectic collection of stemware, she poured a generous serving of a chartreuse carbonated drink. Only after she swallowed a quarter of the glass did she have the urge to offer some wine to her guest.

"Not while I'm on duty, thanks."

She shrugged and swallowed a few more gulps before she felt the muscles in her chest and stomach relax. The headache lingering at the corners of her eyes melted away.

"Do you want some with dinner?"

"I'm invited?"

"I thought I was stuck with you. My shadow, remember?"

He approached the table and surveyed her offering. "I got the distinct impression you weren't happy with that arrangement. That's why I suggested you call Drew. I didn't know that was a sore spot. I'll take iced tea, if you have it."

She grabbed a pitcher from behind the milk, surmising that Brandon had indeed been traveling the world too long if he thought there was a Southerner alive who didn't keep a fresh pitcher of sweet tea in the back of the fridge. As she poured him a glass, she also realized Brandon probably expected more from a meal than lettuce leaves dotted with poached white meat, mandarin orange segments and carrot, and drizzled with spicy ginger dressing. She pulled a Tupperware of Miss Lily's fried chicken out of the refrigerator and plopped the cold, golden-brown contents onto a platter. Her mother's cook and constant companion had an annoyingly wonderful habit of using her key to fill Serena's cupboards and fridge with more than the healthy fare she served at the spa.

"Drew's not a sore spot. I care about Drew more than anyone. He's my best friend."

Like you used to be.

Brandon slid himself into a chair and filled his plate

with two chicken legs, three wings, a breast and a thigh, apparently not bothered by the future of her marital status enough for his appetite to be dampened much. When she shook her head with disbelief, he scooped some salad onto the side.

"Have you told Drew about the notes?"

"No," she answered forcefully. "I didn't think it was necessary."

"He's your best friend and wants to marry you, but you don't tell him when your life is threatened?"

She filled her plate with a generous helping of salad, then speared a mouthful with her fork. While she chewed, she decided that now definitely wasn't the time to admit she'd fabricated the notes to enlist his help. Despite their intimate conversation in the hallway outside the restaurant, the gulf between them remained as wide as the waterway between Louisiana and Florida, with just as many rough waves and swirling storms. She needed time to figure out the best way to navigate without swamping her future entirely.

"I didn't tell anyone but you. I don't want everyone overreacting. It's all a hoax. Someone's idea of a joke."

"What makes you so sure?"

He didn't wait for her to respond. Instead, he took a bite of the cold chicken and then closed his eyes to savor the combination of spices and breading and juicy meat that made Miss Lily the best cook in all of New Orleans.

A knock at the door waylaid Serena's answer, but she hesitated nonetheless. Lying wasn't her forte and contradicted her daily goal of achieving simplicity and balance in every aspect of her life.

So just what was she doing having dinner with Brandon Chance? Pretending to be a damsel in distress—of all things—in a nonsensical, if not potentially faultless, scheme to divest herself of an unwanted suitor while retaining a cherished friendship? Maybe two?

Maybe everyone was right. Maybe she was crazy.

She scooted out her chair, responding to the second, more insistent rap on the door.

Brandon tore off another mouthful of chicken and stopped her with a greasy hand. "Let me."

She didn't argue. She was too stunned by the direction of her own thoughts to protest what was essentially a smart move for a professional bodyguard.

"That's probably Samantha," she called. "She left a message at the spa saying she'd be stopping by with some stuff."

When the knock sounded again, Serena leaned around from her chair to see Brandon still in the living room, coolly assessing the best way to get around Maurice, who stood sentinel in the foyer, his tail furiously swiping a spot of hardwood and his front paws dancing on the rug. He was better than a peephole. No bark meant the person on the other side of the door was someone he knew. The wagging tail further indicated that the knocker had once, and would probably again, engage the dog in some sort of play.

She left the table, squeezed by Brandon, grabbed the dog's collar with one hand and reached around his mass of fur with the other to open the door. "Hey, Sammie, come on in."

Serena stepped back and held the door wide, and the dog in place, while her sister struggled with an armful of packages.

"I could use a little help," Sammie groused.

"I'm holding the door, aren't I?" Serena answered.

"Here, let me."

Brandon moved between Serena and the wall, his body sliding against hers so quickly and efficiently, she shouldn't have noticed. But she did notice. She and every nerve ending from the tips of her breasts to the rings on her toes. That scent that was his alone, now mixed with the spicy aroma of fresh fried chicken, made him the ultimate comfort food. Her mouth watered. Luckily, Sammie made such a production out of carrying in her boxes, no one seemed to notice her reaction but her.

"Brandon?"

Sammie slid the boxes into his arms, retaining a small flat one on top to carry herself. She assessed him from head to toe, not bothering to hide a wide-eyed reaction of feminine approval.

"Damn," Sammie concluded. "You sure as hell grew up nice."

"Samantha," he acknowledged with a wry grin, shifting the boxes into a straighter, more manageable column. "Now I can be *bewitched* by both Deveaux sisters."

Samantha snorted. "I haven't heard that joke since before Daddy moved out. And there was a good reason for that."

"Not funny?" he answered, grinning.

Samantha pulled out her straightest face. "Not unless you want me to start calling you Derwood."

Serena released Maurice, who bounded over to Sammie joyfully. Brandon had greeted each old friend he'd run into with the same enthusiasm—first Drew, now Sammie—everyone except her.

"I'll pass." He shifted the boxes to the side, facing Samantha as he spoke. "When did you swim back upstream? Aunt Tillie claimed you were going to be the next Linda Hamilton or Sigourney Weaver once your father found you the right part."

"*Your* aunt Tillie listens too much to *my* mother." Samantha gave Maurice a nip of a kiss on the nose, then picked up a brightly covered ball from beneath the secretary and flung it into the kitchen. The dog bounded away, nearly clipping Brandon at the knees. "I never intended to act. My screen time was limited to stunt work."

"Sounds exciting. Why are you back here?"

"Let's just blame it on one too many broken bones and leave it at that, okay?" She tucked her box underneath one arm and balanced a fist on her hip. "Unless you want to end all the speculation simmering through the Quarter and tell us both why you retired from the army?"

His answer was a noncommittal, yet decidedly negative grunt. Then his mouth curved into a friendly smile. "Welcome back."

Samantha grinned. "Right back at you. So, what are you doing hanging around my sister? Hungry for trouble so soon?"

Brandon's chuckle so rankled Serena she hoped he threw out his back standing there with an armful of boxes. Or got a hernia. When he dropped the cardboard containers onto the floor near the kitchen, she realized they were neither heavy nor cumbersome enough to cause this man to even break a sweat.

"Trouble and Serena do go hand in hand, don't they?" he surmised.

"That's what I'm told." Sammie slid her lone package onto an end table and headed toward dinner. "Heard today that she nearly got run over after I dropped her off at your office."

"Who told you that?" Serena asked, protest grinding her voice. She should know better than to think no one witnessed her and Brandon's tumble.

"Mother. Who else?" Sammie answered.

"How did she find out?" Serena threw a suspicious glance at Brandon.

"Don't look at me." Brandon shoved his hands in his pockets. "The last person I'm going to call is your mother, unless I want to hold a séance to figure out who's threatening you."

"Threatening you?" Samantha shot back into the room, gripping a drumstick and licking grease from her lips. "Serena, you told me nothing was wrong."

"Nothing is wrong!" She threw up her hands, swung past her sister and returned to her place at the table. "Unless I count the two of you jumping to conclusions and assigning nefarious intentions to my carelessness. I simply wasn't looking where I was going."

Serena waited for Brandon to tell Sammie about the threats, or that she'd hired him to be her bodyguard, but he did neither. Instead, he sidled over to the casket she'd put on the shelf, surreptitiously shut the lid and came back into the kitchen.

Sammie eyed them both, took another bite of her chicken, chewed and then concluded, "I didn't come over to lecture you on street safety." She swallowed and then licked her fingers. "But don't be surprised if Endora pops in later."

Serena groaned, and pushed away from the table to

quickly grab the phone. The last thing she needed tonight was her mother. Actually, the last thing she needed tonight was her mother knowing Brandon was staying in her house—provided that she didn't already know, either through psychic means or because the neighbors felt obliged to give her a call. The citizens of the French Quarter would by no means be morally outraged by her choice of guests, but they sure as heck wouldn't be able to let such a scintillating tidbit pass without spreading the word to their latest and most beloved queen since Marie Leveau.

Serena couldn't lie to her mother in person. Endora LaCroix Deveaux was a force to be reckoned with in just about every dimension she claimed to visit. And while Serena wasn't sure if Endora's reputed "powers" were more than a heightened sense of intuition or a true psychic phenomenon, she did know without a doubt that Endora *always* knew when she was up to something. And she wouldn't have any qualms about calling her on it in front of Brandon. With no illusions that she could keep her plan secret if Endora walked through the door, she punched in her mother's number.

As Serena dialed, Sammie slid into the chair next to Brandon, eyed then dismissed the salad that didn't have nearly enough sesame oil or clumps of cheese to pique her appetite. She fished a wing from beneath a breast on the platter while Serena thanked Miss Lily for the chicken and asked to speak to Endora.

"You're calling me so I won't come over," her mother said by way of greeting.

"Yes, ma'am, I am." No sense in arguing that point. "I wasn't looking where I was going, but I'm fine. No scratches, no bruises. But if you'd like, I'll stop by and show you."

Endora's laugh was light. "I'd be delighted if you came by, but I know you're fine—physically. I'm not so sure about what's going on in your head."

That makes two of us, Serena thought.

"My head is fine, too." She ran her hand through her hair as Sammie and Brandon looked up from their food. "I'm in the middle of dinner, though, so can I come by in the morning?"

Endora chuckled. "Miss Lily is peeling potatoes as we speak. Tell Brandon not to fill up too much on chicken or he'll miss out on his favorite hash."

Serena winced. Having a psychic for a parent was something she should be used to by now, but she wasn't. Lying and keeping secrets weren't something she did on a daily basis. She hung up the phone after saying goodbye then took another long draught of soda.

"So, how is your mother?" Brandon asked.

"She said not to fill up on chicken 'cause Miss Lily is making that andouille hash you like so much."

"But you didn't tell her..." His protest died off and he shook his head with a resigned frown that slowly turned into a reluctant grin. He picked up a fried thigh and took a big bite.

She and Sammie filled the silence with conversation, mostly about Samantha's quest for gainful employment that didn't require her to prop her eyes open with toothpicks. After a lifetime of jumping off high-rise buildings and driving flaming cars off bridges while the cameras rolled, arranging shoot schedules for the local film board wasn't cutting it.

"Are you going to quit?" Serena asked.

Sammie rolled her now-bare chicken bones into her paper napkin. "As soon as I find something better. I do have to pay the bills."

"A Deveaux in need of money? That's a first." Brandon scooped another helping of Serena's healthy, yet surprisingly tasty salad onto his plate. Growing up in a family of gamblers and speculators, Brandon learned very young not to rely on his parents for money and to keep a rainy-day stash somewhere safe. The military had paid him well for his piloting skills, and with the addition of "danger pay," and no family or household to support, he'd created a hefty portfolio he now needed to learn to spend. But the Deveaux clan controlled a fortune that dated back to the Louisiana Purchase and hadn't stopped increasing since. "Your father is loaded and your mother's not exactly panhandling at Jackson Square."

"You left out the part about me being an adult, Brandon." Samantha explained. "Their money is their money. I need my own."

Serena and Sammie exchanged a quick but meaningful glance that stirred Brandon's interest for an instant—until he pushed the curiosity aside. He had enough Deveaux mysteries to unravel at the moment, not the least of which was the reemergence of his desire for Serena.

Thankfully, he'd learned in the service to present an emotion-free veneer. Piloting helicopters into dangerous territory on covert missions, he knew success depended on him keeping his natural apprehension shielded from his men. The skill served him well when Serena not only admitted she wasn't engaged to Drew, but that she considered his old rival just a friend. He'd felt a leap in the pit of his chest that shocked even him. Given a little time and the distraction of finding out the identity of Serena's cliché-loving pen pal, he'd squash his emotions back into submission where they belonged. But until then, he was having a hell of a good time watching Serena eat and talk and laugh. She was a captivating, beautiful woman, an innately feminine creature that men like him couldn't help but watch.

Looking was all he would do. All he was paid to do. Touching was most definitely out of the question. He'd done so only briefly when she was slicing the bread and again when they answered the door, and his body still thrummed from the feel of her warm skin against his. Touching her again would most definitely lead to kissing, which would inevitably progress to lovemaking. They weren't kids anymore.

But one thing still hadn't changed. He wanted to marry and settle down. Serena wanted to remain free and unfettered. And while he neither envied nor belittled her plans for her future, he knew that making love with Serena would mean something—a promise of sorts. A promise he couldn't keep.

"Sammie knows I'll loan her money if she needs it," Serena said, interrupting his thoughts and giving him a much-needed distraction. "That's not the point. She needs to do something she loves."

"Like?" Brandon asked, suddenly anxious for more chatter.

Sammie tabled her hands and leaned her chin on her knuckles. "Being a bodyguard sounds interesting." She batted her eyelashes with complete and utter abandon. "Need a partner?"

"Ha!"

Serena and Samantha tag-teamed him with serious, pointed stares, jabbing the humor of her suggestion right out of him. "It's not you, of course," he began by way of damage control. The last thing he needed was an argument—in deluxe Deveaux surround-sound—about sexism or selfishness or lack of lifelong loyalties. "I'm too new at this to train someone with no experience."

"Who says I have to be trained? Bodyguarding isn't brain surgery. I know how to shoot a gun, I have a third-degree black belt in tae kwon do and I'm very observant," Sammie concluded. "I had bodyguards around me all the time in L.A."

It was Brandon's turn to frown. She really didn't think his job was a piece of cake, did she? Sure, his first job in New Orleans hadn't exactly gotten under way enough for him to talk about the dangers and intricacies of his career, but he had some stories from Miami that would curl that California-blond hair of hers into tight little ringlets sure to yank her scalp.

"The state of Louisiana says you have to be trained," he told her. "And I'm not just hired muscle. This job requires several licenses and courses. I'm an investigator as well as a personal-protection specialist. Why don't you look into it? Do some research?"

"And then get back to you?" Samantha asked hopefully. Her cat-in-the-cream expression made him wonder if she hadn't just baited him on purpose. Sisters! Obviously, their separate childhoods hadn't diminished their mutual love for manipulation.

Anyway, Brandon didn't need a partner. And he most certainly didn't need a partner whose last name was Deveaux. Though he hardly knew Samantha since she grew up with her father on the West Coast, he felt qualified to draw conclusions based solely on her sibling. Deveaux were unpredictable. Resourceful but unreliable. And flighty as all get-out. Once he discovered who was threatening Serena and neutralized the danger, he'd be done with her *and* her insane pack of relatives.

"There's no harm in us having a talk, but don't get your hopes up. After working in a regiment for eleven years, I'm actually looking forward to going this venture alone."

Samantha's smile dimmed, but didn't diminish enough to let him think for one minute he was off the hook. Her eyes, a darker shade of green than her sister's, still glimmered with plans-in-the-making.

"Well, on that note, I'd better leave you two to whatever you were doing." She slid away from the table, tossed the napkin in the trash under the sink and washed her hands. "Do I want to know what you're doing?" she asked while drying her fingers with a crisp paper towel.

"We're having dinner," Serena answered way too quickly. Brandon saw the light of interest brighten in Samantha's eyes, but she shrugged in acceptance and waved goodbye.

Brandon had no intention of buying Serena's pacifications so easily. If she was indeed lying to him about something, as he suspected, then his attraction to her was blinding him more than failing eyesight ever did. And he was going to do something about it. Right away.

BRANDON LEFT SERENA alone with Maurice at her side, rummaging through the boxes Sammie had delivered, while he hurried to his new apartment to grab clean clothes. As promised, he returned in less than fifteen minutes, hardly enough time for her to sort through her conflicting thoughts and instincts. The Quarter was a relatively small place and the room he'd rented above an old friend's bar on Bourbon Street wasn't more than a quick jaunt from her house on St. Philip. By the time he returned, she still didn't know when or even if she was going to come clean.

"Find anything interesting?" He dug his hands into his pockets, eyeing the mounds of clothes and trinkets she'd spread across the sofa. An odd mix of confusion and intimidation painted his expression while he watched her pick through the treasures. Women's clothing did that to men, especially the kind Sammie was obviously anxious to get rid of. Beaded gowns worn once and only once to various award ceremonies. Trendy designer duds with tags still tucked in the sleeve.

Serena lifted a completely see-through sheath of the filmiest chiffon she'd ever seen. She held it up and eyed Brandon through the swirling shades of burgundy, rust and gold dyed into the fabric. "Define *interesting*."

Brandon cleared his throat and started poking in a box of hats and purses that looked decidedly safer. "Your sister has *interesting* taste in clothes."

Sensing a chink in his indifferent armor, Serena held the incredibly alluring dress up to her body. The spaghetti straps were little more than woven thread and the hem just breezed over the top of her thighs when she sat up onto her knees. Where her sister wore this was beyond her, until she spied the tiny tag hanging from beneath the arm.

Probably another designer "donation" she never got around to showing off. As the daughter of Hollywood's hottest director, Sammie had often been treated like a star herself. The situation wore on her—and Serena totally understood. Living in the shadow of a legendary parent was no easier on the banks of the Mississippi than it was on the shores of the Pacific. But Serena couldn't just up and move. New Orleans was part of her blood, part of her soul.

Just as Brandon once was.

"She does, doesn't she?" She couldn't resist baiting him further, hoping a little teasing would restore her perspective. Old habits were so hard to break. "How do you think I'd look in something like this?"

Brandon's eyes narrowed. "Like a naked woman who paid too much for her dress."

Serena laughed and draped the dress into her "keep" pile. She didn't know why, exactly, but suspected the brief glint of discomfort she'd witnessed in Brandon's expression had something to do with her stashing away the ready-to-not-wear haute couture creation. "You have no imagination, Brandon."

When she glanced up a second later, she was shocked to see the dark intensity in his gaze. Though the dress was nothing more than colored film, she suddenly felt the urge to use it as a shield to block Brandon's incredibly hungry stare. She'd changed into her favorite pajamas—an oversize Mardi Gras T-shirt and leggings—yet for the entire duration of his visual perusal, she felt naked and exposed.

She cleared her throat. "I take it back. Your imagination seems to be working just fine."

Expecting him to laugh at her words, she was met with no reaction. She scooped up the clothes she had no use for and shoved them back in the box. After folding the flaps down, she turned to face his sudden silence and unreadable mien.

"So?" She forced airy brightness into her tone, trying to dispel the discomfort that now hung between them. "Want to help me go through the box of board games?"

His hand snaked out and ensnared her wrist so quickly, she couldn't contain a gasp.

"No. No games. It's time for the truth, Serena. From both of us."

6

BRANDON IMMEDIATELY released her. Was he nuts? If he wasn't before, touching her definitely knocked what was left of his good sense right out of him. The heated, silky skin of her wrist was scented with oils that now clung to his palm, branding him with an essence of lavender, eucalyptus and mint. He ached for more contact.

And that was out of the question.

"Sit down," he ordered, knowing the minute he spoke that he'd chosen the wrong tone. Her dancing green eyes froze midstep.

"Serena, please. Let's just get comfortable."

She chewed on the inside of her lip while she considered his rephrasing. When her eyebrows peaked, she'd clearly decided she was satisfied. She tossed her sister's throwaways aside to make a spot for both of them on the couch.

"Don't you want to shower first?" She eyed the duffel bag he'd leaned against the wall between the kitchen and living room. "Get into your pj's?"

He slid onto the fringed cushions beside her. He should have showered at his apartment. Getting naked in Serena's space had trouble written all over it. "I don't wear pj's."

Watching her for a reaction, he was silently disappointed when she only smirked. "I'd hate to be your neighbor who came knocking in the middle of the night."

"Neighbors shouldn't knock in the middle of the night."

"You're back in the Quarter now. Strange things happen."

"Like threatening notes in your newspaper."

She drew her bare feet up onto the cushions and wrapped her arms around her knees.

Her toenails had sunsets too.

"Stranger than that. What Mrs. Sevilla got on her doorstep from her new husband's first wife...*that* was strange."

Brandon shook his head. He didn't want to know the details. About her neighbors. About her life in this neighborhood. He wanted the facts. The information he needed to finish this job and get the hell out of her life.

Before he started to *really* care for her again. More than he did already. Before he started waking up every morning anticipating when he'd see her or automatically reaching for the phone to call her when he faced a tough challenge or reached a particular milestone. Before he started going to bed at night with her and only her on his mind so that she haunted his dreams with scenarios that could never be real. Like the two of them sharing a future, sharing a life.

After a year in college, he'd convinced himself he was over her forever. Now he realized that separation had simply allowed him the luxury of self-delusion. He still believed he was better off without her—and vice versa—but that logical, commonsense assumption didn't do a damn thing to lessen his desire.

"Serena...the notes. We have to talk about this."

Serena opened her mouth as if ready to answer him with all the detail and minutiae he'd once grown accustomed to. Then she popped her lips together with a smack. "What's to talk about? You find out who sent them, tell them to stop, end of story."

"What about Drew?"

The mention of his name made her twitch. He probably wouldn't have noticed if he hadn't been sitting right beside her. Little by little, she'd crept into his awareness. She couldn't curl her hair around her ear without him noticing. Or chew her bottom lip. Blink. Breathe.

God help him.

"You think he's sending the threats?"

He shrugged his shoulders, thankful to actually talk business for a minute and take his mind off the way her caramel curls caught the amber light of the Tiffany lamp.

"He has motive," Brandon argued.

She grabbed a throw pillow and slipped it between her folded lap and her chest. "Come on, Brandon. Drew wants to marry me, not kill me...though I'm not certain the experiences are all that different."

Brandon stood and walked a few paces away. The coziness of conversing on the couch, her all casual and comfy in her oversize T-shirt and no bra—a detail he couldn't help but notice—didn't lend to focused questioning.

"What do you have against marriage? Your parents divorced a long time ago. Aren't you over that by now?"

She looked up at him, somewhat startled by his bluntness. She answered him in a clipped tone.

"Spoken by a man whose parents are still together." She shifted her position on the couch, pulling the pillow closer to her chest. "I'll admit my parents' divorce instigated my negative appraisal of marriage, but I know that some marriages work wonderfully. I'm happy for people like your parents who truly share each other's lives. Maybe I'm just selfish, but I can't see myself in that situation. Can you?"

With this insurmountable difference of opinion out in the open, Brandon felt safe enough to return to his seat beside her. "Yeah, I can. I'd like the American Dream. Wife, kids, two point three dogs," he joked.

"Don't forget the fence," she added, smiling as she spoke. "White picket is still all the rage, though we don't use them here in the Quarter."

"I don't plan to live in the Quarter."

"Just another thing we don't have in common." She nodded silently, then added, "Isn't it weird? We used to have everything in common."

"Yeah, weird." He mulled over the word and decided *weird* did not accurately describe the situation at all. That he and Serena were so alike—still shared attractions to excitement and thrills and, admittedly, each other—yet held such different visions for themselves was a downright crying shame.

He cleared his throat. "So, Drew knows you don't want to marry him, or anyone, but he's planning everything anyway. Isn't that strange, even to you?"

She smirked at his undisguised insult, but didn't bother to refute it. He'd made it clear long ago that he thought she was odd. For a long time, he'd been drawn to her purely because she saw the world through glasses swirling with bright neon colors and skewed perspectives.

Her annoyance was only for show—just like his teasing.

"Very strange. But I still don't think Drew would send me threatening notes."

"Being in love can make some men desperate," he answered.

She grabbed the wooden casket containing the threatening notes and shoved it at him. "Leave Drew alone. Why don't you look over these again? Dust them for fingerprints or do some fancy paper analysis."

"I might finally have a motive behind these threats and you want to back off? Why?"

"Because this line of thinking is ridiculous. Drew is the guy who flunked biology because he couldn't bring himself to dissect the frog."

"Just because he's threatened you doesn't mean he intends to follow through. Maybe he's trying to scare you, make you think you'll be safer if you marry him."

"That's ridiculous," she muttered.

"Men do ridiculous things sometimes to get what they want, especially when they're in love."

"Drew's not in love with me."

Brandon clutched the inner linings of his pockets and twisted hard, trying to ease some of the frustration her declaration caused. He hated when women assumed they knew everything in a man's heart just because they watched talk shows and read books about Venus and Mars.

"How do you know? Have you ever been in love, Serena?" He bent so close, she had to tilt her head up to meet him eye to eye. "Do you know what love feels like?"

She looked up at him, defiance enhancing her features so he couldn't look away, even if he wanted to. Her eyes caught the dim light of the nearby lamp and turned the golden glow into pure, green fire. Her chin tilted upward; her cheeks flamed. Her mouth, so generous and soft only moments before, now featured lips drawn in an obstinate line.

"Do you?" she demanded.

He struggled to keep his hands in his pockets—no matter how much he wanted to grab her and shake her. Or worse, kiss her. "I asked first."

LOVE FEELS something like this, Serena silently decided. Her heart pounded like a drum in her chest, her nerves thrummed like freshly picked strings of a jazzman's double bass. Standing so close, she couldn't help but breathe in the scent that was decidedly Brandon—pure unfettered musk and man. Basic. Primal. Delicious. Coated by the musty odors of the Quarter's hot asphalt, ancient bricks and fiery spices, he was once again a part of the Vieux Carre—and part of her, like it or not.

"You asked me first? That's an infantile evasion," she pointed out, equally childishly resorting to pointless bickering rather than facing the truth. She could blame Brandon and their lifetime of similar interactions for her response, but that wouldn't be fair. They'd both grown up. They both knew better.

Now they just had to admit it.

He stared, waiting for her response.

"No, Brandon. I don't know what love feels like. Do you?"

Brandon pulled his hands from his pockets and ran them through his hair. She watched the gesture with hungry fascination, her hands anxious to comb through the midnight-dark strands, to brand the texture onto her palms.

"I thought I did. Once," he admitted.

"When?"

As his gaze locked with hers, she knew exactly the moment he referred to. That night. In the gym.

"I was a kid. I didn't know how to show...the girl...how I felt."

"Do you know now?" she asked, closing the space between them. She placed her palm against his chest and marked the time of his beating heart, grinning inside when the rapid tempo matched her own. She and Brandon had decidedly different plans for the future, but denying leftover feelings from the past wasn't going to make them go away.

Confronting those feelings might. And not with words. With action.

"Kiss me, Brandon. Like you should have so long ago."

His pupils dilated, adding a dark shadow to the intensity of his gaze. "You don't know what you're asking."

"Yes, I do. I'm asking you to do what I know you want to. Kiss me," she demanded, then closed her eyes to await his next move.

First, he caressed her cheek with such gentleness, Serena imagined he'd plucked a feather from one of her boas and now used the soft down to tease her skin. She inhaled sharply to keep from gasping, but the added friction of padded callus to her sensitized flesh accelerated her heartbeat and stole her captured breath away.

"We were so young," he whispered. "I was so stupid. But I never told you...even before I got drunk, I wanted to be with you. More than I'd wanted anything."

Don't look. Don't look him in the eye. Her good sense fell deaf to her curiosity. Intending only to take a quick peek to gauge his honesty, she was immediately held prisoner by his intense stare.

"Why didn't you tell me?" she asked. "Then? Or after?"

He licked his lips to cover a bashful grin, but the action only brought more attention to his mouth—a mouth she craved as she craved no other. "How does a guy keep an ounce of pride and admit that to the girl he groped?"

"You're doing it now."

"Time changes things."

"Like you wanting me more than anything?" she asked. She'd asked him to kiss her and still he hadn't. Yet. Maybe he wouldn't. Maybe he no longer wanted to.

He crooked a finger beneath her chin. "Time and distance didn't do much to change that. Damn them both."

He lowered his lips slowly, tentatively, briefly brushing his mouth against hers. He tasted like spicy ginger. Like hot fire.

"Tell me no, Serena." His words were a whispered command, and she knew he would stop if she asked him to. He wouldn't betray her trust a second time, just as she wouldn't let a second opportunity pass to explore the connection between them.

"I can't," she answered, raising herself onto the balls of her bare feet to swipe her lips across his again.

"Good."

He pressed harder this time, enough for her to feel the slick warmth of his lips, the moist heat of his mouth. She slipped her arms around his waist. Hunger beat a path from the pit of her belly to the edge of her tongue. He eased one hand behind her neck, one to the small of her back and met her halfway, pulling her as close as he could while they learned what they'd missed all those years ago.

He was a natural-born leader, a man in command. But not here, not now. He let her set the pace. She snuggled closer, her unbound breasts beneath her T-shirt flush with the hardness of his chest. She made no secret of her responses, moaning softly from the back of her throat.

The instinct to explore, the primal need to feel his skin against her palm and learn the planes of his body, couldn't be denied. She spread her fingers over his chest, then brushed her palms downward.

When she skimmed the top of his waistband, he broke the kiss. Before they went too far? Felt too much? But he didn't release her. Instead, he turned his head aside and buried his nose in her hair.

"You're dangerous, woman."

Serena unfolded herself from his hold and stepped aside. "You're not exactly a day in church yourself." She drew her fingers to her mouth, marveling at the thrumming heat still firing her lips. She couldn't allow this to go any further—at least, not until she'd told him the whole truth.

If he'd been honest with her fifteen years ago, told her how he'd really felt about her, their lives might not have turned out any differently, but Serena knew she would have made other choices in the past few days. She certainly wouldn't have lied to him this morning or schemed to rope him into the mess that was her personal life. She wouldn't have had to.

"I've made a huge mistake," she said. "I shouldn't have hired you to be my bodyguard."

He nodded, smiling, obviously aware that she'd pulled some sort of scam on him. "No, you probably shouldn't have. Care to tell me why you did? And no more bull, Serena. The truth. All of it."

Truth was, she'd used him—or had schemed to—without knowing how he'd truly felt all those years ago, without realizing she might hurt him in precisely the way he'd hurt her. But now wasn't the time to rehash the past. He'd asked about now.

She crossed her arms over her chest and admitted the most basic truth in one breath. "I chose you so Drew would see us together and think we were involved again. He'd be the first person to remind me that mixing friendship and romance leads to disaster."

Brandon grew silent. All expression, all reaction disappeared from his eyes. He'd always had a first-rate poker face, but this one nearly made her shiver.

"Not a bad plan, actually." He stepped aside and grabbed his duffel bag, fingering the canvas strap for a moment before he swung it over his shoulder. "This one, at least, I understand. If Drew warned you away from me, he'd have to see the parallel to his own foolishness. Not a bad plan at all."

Without another word, he headed toward her guest room. Serena reached out to stop him, to explain the rest—from the fake notes to her honest response to his kiss—but stopped. He wasn't going anywhere except to take a shower. She needed time to regroup. Recover from the kiss she'd waited for her entire life.

Immediately after he closed the bathroom door, Serena got to work, determined to clean up the mess she'd created before she went to bed. And she wasn't just thinking about the scattered boxes and strewn clothing. She was thinking about lies and mistruths. Omissions. Things she should have told him this morning. Things she should have told him fifteen years ago, if her wounded pride had only let her. Perhaps the whole truth was better aged, when they were mature enough to appreciate the depth of their adolescent feelings—and knew the limitations of any future they might have.

Brandon wanted a wife and kids and a house in the suburbs. Serena couldn't imagine ever leaving the Quarter or giving up the freedom to dance until daybreak at Restoration Hall or close up the spa on a whim to take a friend to the bayou.

They were the same, yet as different as Lake Pontchartrain and the Mississippi River. And they had no canal to connect them, nothing but the attraction that had only heightened with their kiss.

It was late, near midnight. She let the dog out and watched the clock until the hour hand went one minute past midnight, declaring the end to a dry Tuesday. She fished two glasses from the back of her liquor cabinet and filled them both with a finger of fine, aged bourbon.

She was sitting on the floor amid a neat pile of old board games, sipping the liquor to give her courage and leaning her back against the couch for strength, when Brandon emerged from the bathroom ten minutes later. The edges of his jet-black hair glistened with moisture. His skin radiated the heat of his shower. He wore gray sweatpants that hung low on his waist and a crisp white T-shirt over that military-muscled chest of his.

"Find everything okay?" she croaked, then loosened the walls of her throat with another sip of bourbon.

"Remind me to pick up some unscented shampoo."

"Ylang-ylang is very relaxing."

His smirk denoted his disbelief. "Sleep is relaxing. Don't you think you should be getting some?"

"I'm a night owl. That's why the spa doesn't open till ten."

He tousled his hair once more with a towel, then folded it in sharp thirds and draped it over the bathroom's doorknob. "An advantage of being your own boss."

She lifted the second glass to him. "One of a few."

He shook his head at her proffered drink.

"Tuesday's over, Brandon. One drink. Don't tell me you can't hold your bourbon anymore."

He snorted and reached for the glass. "I can hold my bourbon *and* your bourbon, thank you very much. Still drink it straight up, I see."

"Great-aunt Aggie insisted that real ladies drank their bourbon two ways—in a julep or straight up. I was too lazy to crush the mint."

Though his T-shirt wore its crisp, bleached whiteness like a full-braided dress uniform, his sweatpants were soft and somewhat sloppy. She couldn't help but follow the curves of muscle beneath the athletic gray. Her fingers itched to touch him, to explore and learn about the man she'd thought she knew so well, when in reality she didn't have a clue.

When he turned and squatted to sit beside her on the floor, she drew the drink to her mouth and watched from behind the glass, thankful the odor of strong alcohol would offset—at least temporarily—the powerful essence that was Brandon Chance.

She took a long sip of her drink, savoring the burning flavor as it first assailed her tongue, then her throat and belly. *To fortification,* she silently toasted.

Brandon slid a pile of board games closer and pawed through the collection, all obviously old but surprisingly intact right down to the pewter shoe in Monopoly and the sand-filled timer in Scrabble.

Brandon looked around and took a hearty swig of his bourbon, downing half the serving in one gulp. "What are you, the Salvation Army of the Deveaux clan?"

Serena smirked as she pulled a dusty version of Clue from the stack. "I like old stuff. Sue me."

He smiled when she removed the lid to check the contents. "That brings back a lot of memories." He leaned back against the couch and stretched his legs, causing his impressive thigh muscles to tighten the loose sweatpants. "Miss Scarlet. In the library. With the handcuffs."

"There aren't handcuffs in Clue," she said, pulling

out the wrinkled directions from beneath the playing board.

"You sure?" He leaned sideways to look over her shoulder. "I could have sworn I played a game with Miss Scarlet where she used handcuffs."

When she forced herself to think beyond the effects of his nearness—hot-shower smell and bourbon-laced breath and all—she realized he was teasing her. "That was a fantasy, Brandon. You can't kill a person with handcuffs."

"No, but you can make them beg for mercy."

He wiggled his eyebrows suggestively. His blatant innuendo, coupled with the intoxicating effects of the liquor, made her laugh out loud. He chuckled along with her. The sounds of their laughter imbued the air with a familiarity and comfort Serena hadn't felt in years. Placed alongside her earlier admission that she'd hired him to dissuade Drew, she realized the man had an incredible capacity to forgive.

"Will they help a person beg for absolution?" she wondered, her voice small and unsure. She swallowed the last of her drink and suddenly wished she hadn't put the bottle back in the cabinet. But she hadn't relied on alcohol to give her courage before now—she certainly didn't need it tonight.

"Absolution? For what? For hiring me to help you with two troubles at once? I would have preferred you told me everything from the beginning, but you had good reason to think I wouldn't help you."

Her chuckle lacked humor. "That's an understatement."

The grin slowly faded from his face as he watched her struggle with her conscience.

"Serena, why do I get the feeling you're not telling me everything?"

"It's about the notes," she said.

"The threats on your life?"

She nodded, wincing as he sat up straighter, grabbed her empty glass from her quivering hand and put it beside his on the floor. He still believed her life was in danger. And apparently, he *cared*.

"You're holding something back. Tell me. It could make the difference between life and death. *Your* life and death."

She drew her knees to her chest as her stomach plummeted into the soles of her feet. Fighting the urge to scoot out of his line of reach, she chewed her bottom lip and considered how exactly she should phrase her admission—but all she could think about was the wording of his plea: life and death?

Oh, yeah. Because he was going to kill her.

7

"THE NOTES AREN'T REAL. I'm not in danger. I made it all up."

Brandon listened to her tumbling confession, then huffed out his pent-up exasperation in a rush of breath. Now wasn't the time for her to have second thoughts about hiring him! He shouldn't have kissed her. He shouldn't have once again surrendered to temptation, no matter how willing she'd been or how sweet she'd tasted. He'd hoped the kiss would show her that he cared—then and now—despite his best efforts not to. He certainly hadn't intended to...what? Scare her? Force her to lie now about the notes just to get out of their deal?

"Serena," he said softly, fighting to keep his irritation in check, "forget that you had to dare me into taking this job. Forget that I told you I didn't want it. I wouldn't trust this assignment to anyone else. You don't have to lie to me."

She drew her thumbnails into her mouth and nibbled, then pulled them out quickly before she bit through the acrylic. "I'm not lying. I mean, I'm not lying *now*. But I was. This morning. Two minutes ago, to be accurate."

This time, he listened. Forced himself to process her admission and all the implications. The signs were all there. The averted eyes. The tasty nails. He could only imagine what her teeth were doing to the inside of her mouth.

Grabbing her ankles, he scooted her around to face him.

"Say that one more time," he demanded.

"I made up the notes myself," she answered.

She was telling him the truth—now—and she wasn't enjoying the experience.

"Why?"

"So you'd become my bodyguard."

"You got me with the dare and the bet."

Her eyes grew glossy. She wasn't going to cry—Serena wasn't the type to pull out tears for sympathy—but she was fighting like hell to keep herself together. He knew then that he'd better believe whatever crazy tale she told. Her voice was small, but clear and honest. "I got you to come here on the dare and the bet. I thought that without the notes, without proof, you would have left and not looked back before we had a chance...before..."

The kiss.

He suddenly realized he was touching her. His hands encircled her slim ankles; his palms rested on her smooth, bare insteps. With the reflexes he'd honed in the service, he shot back and forced a safe distance.

No. This could not be happening. Not again. He'd been roped into some convoluted Serena Deveaux scheme unaware and guileless. He'd already accepted that she'd chosen him rather than another bodyguard to make Drew face the futility of his marriage quest, but Brandon had still believed the threats were real. She'd lied about *everything*.

Had she lied about wanting him? About wishing things had turned out differently for them?

About caring?

But why? For revenge? For kicks?

"Thanks for telling me," he said, swallowing his anger, but not his pride. "I'll be going now." Before he wrung her slim, sexy column of a neck.

"No! Brandon, you can't!" She didn't stand, but reached up and grabbed his hands. "Not until you hear why I lied. You know I don't do things without good reason. Never in my whole life have I enlisted your help with something that wouldn't eventually serve the greater good. Think of one time I did—one time—and you can go without another word from me."

Words didn't appeal to him at the moment, but growling served him damn well. He didn't bother trying to think of an instance where her lunacy was for the sake of ill will or simple amusement. He wouldn't find one. Of the two of them, the only one who'd ever acted selfishly was him.

"Why?" He forced the response out on a heated breath and pulled his hands from her grasp.

She swallowed, then stood, lithe and limber in her slim leggings and oversize shirt. Now wasn't the time for him to notice how truly lovely she was—sprightly, alluring, full of the carefree outlook that alluded him all his life—but he couldn't help himself, not when she wore contriteness with all the skill of a penitent schoolgirl.

"I needed you to help me dissuade Drew. I told you that. But there was more. Much more. Something I'm certain I didn't realize until..."

She glanced over her shoulder at the spot where they'd stood when they kissed—when they'd shared an intimacy borne from a long-simmering, age-old desire.

Neither of them wanted to want. Neither of them wanted to feel.

But they had.

Brandon crossed his arms over his chest, grasping for fortification against her shimmering, ocean-green eyes, her cinnamon and magnolia scent. He'd already taken one sucker punch. He braced himself for the rest of the assault.

"Why grift me? To make me pay for what I did to you?"

Her laugh was less than comical, but she didn't waver under the weight of his accusatory glare. Instead, she stepped closer and laid her hands on his crossed arms, tucking her fingers against his chest. "I don't do revenge anymore, Brandon. I did pull a scam, but believe me, I pulled it on me more than you."

Of their own volition, his muscles eased. His ire cooled a notch while the surface of his skin—precisely where she touched him—ignited with instant fire. He struggled to hold on to his anger, clenching his fists tighter and grinding his teeth.

"What is that supposed to mean?"

She stared at him intently, as if he should know the answer to that question without thinking, as if it was something as obvious as the color of the sky or the name of the city in which he now lived.

"I know Aunt Tillie told you all about my social life while you were gone. Didn't you ever wonder, just once, why I never had a serious relationship?"

As she spoke, she skimmed her fingers over his skin, plucking the dark hair on his arms, imbuing his flesh with her body heat, her scent. His nostrils flared. Need stirred in his groin, but if she felt him harden when she brushed her belly against him, she didn't reveal an ounce of surprise.

"You've never been big on commitment," he answered, knowing that wasn't entirely true. Serena shunned the institution of marriage, but she knew all about loyalty and unconditional love and friendship. If he'd stuck around after graduation, or if he'd just given her the opportunity, she would have found a way to restore the trust they'd lost that night. It was her way, her nature.

With ease, she uncrossed his arms, grazed her palms from his biceps to his wrists, then wrapped his hands around her waist.

"I couldn't want anyone when I still wanted you."

So simple. So honest. Brandon stood there, shell-shocked. Unable to move, even when she raised her lips slowly, tentatively, briefly brushing her mouth against his in an exploratory sweep—a recognizance sortie of the most dangerous kind. The scent of spice and flower and pure, unfettered woman swirled around her, catching him like a tailwind, sending him into a spiral he didn't know how to maneuver.

"Touch me, Brandon."

"No," he answered.

His heart chopped in his chest like the blades of his favorite Little Bird aircraft. Hard and strong, yet deceptively silent. She wouldn't know how excited she made him, so long as he exercised the full breadth of his self-control.

"Why? Because you won't marry me in the morning? That's your dream, not mine. I just want you. I always have."

She pressed against his mouth harder this time, unafraid, bold, acting on pure want and desire. She paid no heed to the consequences. She lived for the thrill. And he might have broken away had she not slipped her arms around his waist and up beneath his T-shirt, pressing him closer, opening her mouth and teasing his lips with her supple tongue.

She was willing to take a risk. How could he, a Chance, do anything less?

Besides, he needed to touch her, taste her, make her his—even temporarily—as he'd never needed anything in his life.

He folded his arms inward, releasing her waist and sliding his hands up and across her cheeks, then into her hair, bending her back as he moved, taking control of the kiss. The taste of bourbon lingered in her mouth, the distilled fire intensified by the heat of her tongue and lips clashing with his. She kissed him with no reservations, opening her mouth wide, teasing his teeth with her tongue, gripping him closer and closer until they nearly lost their balance.

She should have been born a Chance the way she tempted fate and good sense in pursuit of pure, unadulterated lust and need. How could he deny her? How could he deny himself? He wanted her, always had. And now she offered herself, with no strings, no promises.

But he knew too well the consequences of acting on impulse, on sheer need. He'd touch her—yes. He was powerless to stop himself. But he'd draw the line...somewhere.

With a careful spin, he lowered himself onto the couch and drew her down with him, folding her onto his lap. She whimpered when he settled her sideways, so she no longer pressed against his erection. He'd done that for his own sanity, but she didn't appreciate the gesture. Instead, she whipped her leg around and straddled him.

"What are you afraid of?" she challenged.

He tilted an eyebrow and considered disclaiming any fear at all, but then decided she knew him too well to believe him.

"Once I start, I won't be able to stop."

She scooted closer, pressing her breasts to his chest and raking her hands through his hair while she bathed his face and neck in hot, wet kisses. "Then don't stop."

Serena appreciated Brandon's innate sense of honor, but if he didn't touch her soon, she'd go mad with wanting. She'd fought her lust for him and lost. Deveaux dealt with failure much better than Chances did. True to her own family name, she'd make the most of this defeat, then sustain herself on the memory long after he walked out her door.

Grabbing the hem of her T-shirt, she moved to toss it over her head, when Brandon stopped her. He slipped the material out of her grasp and guided her hands to his shoulders.

"Going too fast got me in trouble last time, *chère*."

She gripped his shoulder hard at the sound of the endearment, at the unexpected return of that subtle Cajun accent he'd abandoned at West Point. She searched his eyes, dark and pewter and stormy, and witnessed the return of the boy he once was—wild and unpredictable as the bayou—packaged in the body of a man who had more control than a fifteen-foot-high levee and more power than the Mississippi itself.

He slipped his hands beneath her bottom and eased her upward, brushing his lips against her breasts through her shirt, exhaling his hot breath so her nipples flared and gave him his target.

He flicked his tongue across the tight nub. She gasped at the mixed sensations of moist heat and soft cotton. Sliding her hands around his neck, she snuggled closer, offered more. "Slow is all well and good, but you're making me crazy."

His grin was unadulterated pleasure.

"Seems fair, under the circumstances, don't you think? You *did* lie to me."

The feel of his hardness between her legs, thick and accessible beneath his elastic waistband, made her want only to touch him. To explore this explosive sensuality unhampered by talk or excuses or explanations.

"I lied to you because I didn't know the truth. I didn't know how much I wanted to be with you—still. And unless you can come up with a damn good reason why we shouldn't, could you please just shut up and kiss me?"

So enticing. So tempting. Brandon did as she asked, slipping his hands beneath her shirt, running them up her back, then beneath her arms, teasing the outer swells of her breasts with his thumbs while their mouths mated. She cooed and hummed, letting him know what pleased her, urging him to go farther, touch deeper, with the sounds of her gratification, with the grinding of her hips to his, with the full breadth of her luscious mouth.

On a second sweep beneath her shirt, he allowed himself to graze her nipples. She cried out, so sensitive, so tuned with her body, with her needs. Before he could stop her, she ripped her shirt away.

The sight of her stole his breath. She was lovely. Round and soft, yet slim and hard. Beyond any teenage fantasy. Beyond any adult dream.

And she was his for the taking.

But for what? One night? One evening of pleasure? And then? Brandon mentally shook himself. What the hell was he doing? Hadn't he spent years relearning, harnessing his natural instincts, mastering the art of looking before he leaped.

"Brandon? What's wrong? You don't like what you see?"

She sensed his hesitation. Attempted a joke. He smiled in natural response, kissed her, and as much as it tore him in two, slipped her off his lap and handed her her discarded shirt.

He couldn't do this. It wasn't right. Not in the way that counted. Pandering without thought to his own wants and needs—even if she seemingly wanted and needed the very same thing—was wrong. Serena was his client. And more than that, she was his friend again. His first responsibility was to keeping her safe. Her Cliché-Killer threats may have been bogus, but he posed a danger all too real.

He'd hurt her once before by not living up to her expectations. And since he knew they couldn't have a future together, he couldn't cause that same pain again. She may have claimed to want nothing from him, but she'd been wrong about her own heart before. They needed time, distance.

"I'm your bodyguard, Serena. My job is to protect you."

She crossed her arms, barely covering her breasts, barely hiding the dark, aroused peaks of her nipples or the dark, aroused desire in her eyes.

"I made up the threats, remember? I'm not in danger."

He stood up and spun, pointing both fingers at her, shaking them for a moment while he formulated his argument. "You're wrong, Serena. Dead wrong. If you weren't in danger before, you are now. And I have only one maneuver to stop it."

Turning, he scanned the room and reestablished his bearings, growing angry as he realized the full impact of their kiss on his ability to function. He'd gone too far, risked too much. Even for a Chance.

"Where are you going?" she asked, though thankfully, she didn't follow.

He forced himself out of the living room, into the guest room to retrieve his duffel bag then back toward the front door and sweet, sweet freedom. She didn't need his services. And he didn't need this complication. As he scooped the tan canvas strap onto his shoulder, he focused on his future—and her future—and how the two would never work as one.

"I'll rip up your check first thing in the morning." He turned and faced her, wanting to say more but knowing no words could possibly suffice. She'd been right when she said that her deception to break her engagement was born of good intentions. But he couldn't be a part of it. Serena represented everything he'd worked for fifteen years to gain in his life: control over his basic instincts, a taming of his natural need for danger and risk and uncertainty. And what he couldn't subdue, he channeled into positive undertakings, like his time in the service or his new job.

But nothing good could come of his kissing Serena again—nothing positive would result from him learning where to touch her to make her moan or where to kiss her to make her shout his name in ecstasy.

Nothing but complete and utter bliss...along with complete and utter disaster.

"I can't help you," he said, just to make sure she understood.

Her eyes narrowed to slits of glossy green. She shrugged back into her shirt, leaving her hair in sexy disarray and nearly distracting him from seeing the anger in her glare.

"Keep the money, Brandon!" She dug her hands onto her hips, daggers of betrayal darkening her gaze. "If you're half the idiot I think you are right now, you're going to need that cash to find a new line of work."

"Idiot? Me? Walking away right now is going to be the smartest thing I've ever done." He jabbed the air with his finger. "You know it! Do Drew a favor, Serena. Break his heart. In the long run, he'll thank you. Trust me."

The sound of crashing glass, immediately followed by Serena's high-pitched scream, stopped his tirade. He tossed his duffel and shot toward her in one movement, glancing over his shoulder to see the sparkling shards of her front window rain down onto the parlor furniture.

"Get down," he ordered, even as Serena covered her face and ducked beside the couch. He curved his body over hers until he heard the last tinkle of glass fall on the hard wood.

Then nothing. No car engine. No footfalls on the sidewalk. Just silence until Maurice started barking from the back porch.

"You okay?" he asked, scanning the room.

"What was that?"

"Stay down."

He remained crouched as he explored the floor, glad he'd thrown on his shoes after his shower or else his feet would be bleeding from remnants of glass. He found the projectile quickly—a large red brick, wrapped with brown paper.

"What do you see?"

He ignored her question while he snapped the rubber band that held the torn piece of grocery bag around the brick. He read the message and shook his head.

Not surprisingly, Serena had scooted as near as she could in her shoeless feet. "What is that?"

He turned, careful to keep his balance amid the jagged glass. Holding up the note, he watched her eyes scan the perfectly placed vinyl letters.

"This is impossible," she claimed.

He turned the paper and read the words aloud. "'Better safe than dead.' Sounds like your Cliché Killer to me."

"But there is no Cliché Killer!"

Moving to the window, he scanned the street. Except for a few neighbors emerging from their homes to investigate the ruckus, nothing suspicious caught his eye. Whoever delivered the message was more than likely long gone, leaving him with not only Serena and his rejuvenated attraction to her to deal with, but a mystery as well.

"Obviously, there is now."

8

BRANDON CLOSED the door behind the police sergeant,
once again promising to apprise him of any develop-
ments, including new threats. Though the seasoned officer had first distrusted Brandon because of his profession, the Quarter-born officer gave him the benefit of
the doubt when he realized he'd once won a huge
amount of money at a gaming table when his Aunt Tillie was dealing. The French Quarter was a small com-
munity peopled with tourists and drifters at all hours
of the day and night, but strangers were difficult to
find among the locals.

"I should call my mother," Serena announced. She'd
sat in the same spot on the corner of the couch through-
out the entire parade of neighbors and police, answering questions just as he'd instructed her—revealing
only what had happened with the shattered window
and nothing about her ruse with the fake notes. Brandon couldn't see any point to such explanations except
to prove that Serena was indeed as wacky as most people believed her to be.

Personally, Brandon no longer cared if Serena was
certifiably insane. She was in danger. That's all that
mattered.

"Let your mother's spirit guides tell her in a dream.
I'm going to clean up this mess and you're going to
take a shower."

She wrinkled her nose at him, her sense of humor damaged but not destroyed. "Why? Do I smell?"

God, yes, he thought. Like cinnamon and magnolia and the spicy, exotic essence of a woman born and bred amid the voodoo influence of the Quarter. The elixir was the most powerful magic Brandon had ever encountered, and something deep inside told him there was no gris-gris to ward off the effects.

"You need to relax while I tape up that window."

He watched her walk toward her bedroom, looking like a scout that had somehow stumbled into a secret enemy camp. Stunned. Frightened. Uncertain of what had happened before and what would happen next. When he heard the click of her door, followed by the bang of a few drawers and then the running of water, he went looking for a broom.

By the time he'd finished sweeping and vacuuming, then had cut the boxes Samantha had brought to cover the windows, Serena emerged from the bedroom dressed in a similar T-shirt and leggings as she'd had on before, though she looked decidedly more exhausted and slightly damp. She padded silently to the kitchen, opened the back door without looking first and whistled. Maurice bounded onto the porch, but she grabbed his collar before he bounced over the threshold.

"Is that glass all cleaned up?" she asked.

"Did the best I could," he answered, "but maybe he shouldn't come in here until we have better light."

She nodded and led the dog back onto the porch where he heard her lock the doggie flap on the screen door.

"It's a cool night," she declared when she returned. "He can sleep outside. Have you seen the cat?"

Oh, he'd seen the cat all right. After he finished vacuuming, he'd heard a scratching in the front bedroom. When he investigated, he'd come face-to-face with a massive Himalayan—a ball of beige and brown fur with eyes so blue they practically glowed in the dark. If his aunt Tillie hadn't reported last summer that Endora's cat—the feline he'd shared mutual hate with his entire childhood—had finally kicked the old-age bucket, he would have thought he'd seen a ghost.

"She fled to the pantry about ten minutes ago. I take it she's related to that monster your mother tormented me with as a child."

The comment succeeded in tugging a small smile from her sullen expression.

"Tabitha wasn't the friendliest cat in the world. Tabitha II is much more people-oriented, once you get to know her."

"No, thanks. I don't trust cats."

"That says more about you than I think you want to, Brandon," she teased. Her smile faded the minute she saw the cardboard-covered windows. Without another word, she turned back into the kitchen.

With almost mindless automation, Serena took a small bowl from the cupboard, filled it with one tablespoon of canned cat food mixed with a generous helping of kibble. She set the food just inside the pantry, a walk-in space separated from the kitchen by a coordinating floral-patterned drape, then washed her hands and the spoon, finally turning to look at Brandon with vacant expectation.

Tell me what to do next was written all over her face,

and this wasn't an expression he was accustomed to seeing on her—ever. Serena took care of herself. She made her own choices, her own decisions. Anything he convinced her to do was usually based on a strong presentation or an irresistible dare.

He glanced at the wall clock hanging above the sink. Midnight had come and gone. No matter how much he wanted to begin unraveling the twisted web of Serena's initial plan and this new, unexpected episode, he couldn't ignore the utter exhaustion stooping her shoulders and darkening the skin beneath her suddenly sunken eyes.

She was afraid, an emotion Brandon bet big bucks she'd never truly felt before. And the experience had wiped her out.

"Why don't you go to bed? I'll turn off all the lights and check the doors and windows. We can talk in the morning."

She nodded, wordlessly scuffling in her fuzzy blackcat slippers toward her bedroom. She turned before entering and forced a small smile. "Does this mean you're back on the job?"

"I didn't get a chance to rip up that check," he answered, leaning against the vacuum he hadn't yet stored in the front closet. "But I'm just a bodyguard, Serena. Nothing more."

She nodded again, the shock of actually experiencing an unexpected threat against her life obviously kicking her desire for him right out of her. For that, Brandon was glad. He had enough on his plate protecting her from the threats. Protecting her from *him* seemed above and beyond his capabilities.

SERENA AWOKE to the aroma of freshly brewed, strong chicory coffee and spicy andouille sausage. Sounds of whispered conversations and the sizzling of breakfast disappeared when she closed the bathroom door, but when she reemerged scrubbed and brushed and looking a lot better than she expected after only a few hours of fitful sleep, she heard her mother's distinctive Creole accent echoing in the kitchen.

"And exactly what are you going to do about this?"

Disguised by understated annoyance, Brandon's reply simmered with a childhood's worth of conflict and disbelief. "Why don't you look in your crystal ball and tell me, Endora?"

"Disrespectful! It's a wonder the military didn't teach you some manners."

"Isn't this just like old times?" Serena hurried into the kitchen, leaned over her mother and kissed her forehead then did the same to Miss Lily, who kept watch over the stove. She avoided greeting Brandon. How does one say good morning to the man who haunted you nearly all night—asleep and awake?

"You'd think they'd learn to like each other after all these years," Miss Lily lamented, her dark-coffee skin stretched over a wide, indulgent smile.

Serena inhaled the heavenly scent of Miss Lily's cooking. The mingled scents of the trinity—onion, green pepper and celery—mixed with potent garlic, meaty sausage and hearty potato, created a breakfast delicacy Serena indulged in only on special occasions. Since her mother and Brandon had been in a room together without her to referee for nearly a quarter of an hour and they were both still alive, Serena deemed a party was definitely in order.

"If they ever learn to like each other, I'm certain the universe will implode and leave the rest of us adrift in space." Another point to add to her growing list of reasons why tricking Brandon into becoming her bodyguard was the worst idea she'd come up with since she convinced the drama department to stage *The Best Little Whorehouse in Texas* as the senior musical at her Catholic high school. She'd stayed awake half the night composing that list in her mind, the other half wondering who'd thrown the brick through her window. Growing up in the Quarter, Serena had come to consider most strangers as potential friends. She enjoyed people, trusted them—and trusted her ability to sort the good from the bad.

Still, the fact remained that in order for someone to copy her fake threats, they'd have to have broken into her home, sorted through her personal belongings, then decided to take up where her ruse left off—all for reasons she couldn't fathom. Last night, the idea terrified her. In the light of day, she was madder than hell.

But for now, she had her mother and Brandon to worry about. Keeping them from strangling each other was inherently more important than catching the maniac who'd tried—*tried*, she emphasized—to unravel her hard-earned sense of peace.

She leaned over the sizzling cast-iron skillet and took a great big whiff, hoping to dispel the disquiet churning inside her. "I don't suppose you could figure out a way to make tofu smell that good? I could make a mint at the spa."

Miss Lily laughed as she always did, shaking her head and undoubtedly wondering how Serena, after growing up on her old-style Cajun cooking, could possibly have developed an actual liking for healthy fare. They'd had this conversation a million times, and the familiarity of Lily's perplexed expression banished some of Serena's lingering fear and confusion.

But then she had Brandon's kisses to deal with. The first kiss had been so gentle, so soft and sensual and sizzling with years of unrequited desire—his and hers both. With one brief touching of lips, he'd transported them back to the night of graduation and undone all the heartbreak and anger and hurt.

Then like a fool, she'd spurred him to go farther, to risk more than the new Brandon could—more than was wise and controlled and part of his master plan. He'd pulled away, and it was her fault for going too far too fast. If not for some sicko making a real threat on her life, he would have left, the opportunity to explore the fullness of their passion gone forever.

She shrugged, determined to find means to remedy his reluctance just as soon as they figured out who the heck had sent her that threat. Like it or not, Brandon would insist he solve her mystery before dealing with the attraction still simmering between them.

But they would deal with it. She'd make sure of that.

"So, Serena," her mother sang after a long sip of coffee, "when were you going to tell me you were being stalked?"

Serena grabbed a mug from the cupboard, glancing over her shoulder at Brandon, who rolled his eyes. He'd obviously given up that piece of information in his explanation of his presence in her house so early in the morning.

"None of the threats were real—I mean, really dangerous—until last night." She grabbed the aluminum pot warming on the stove and poured a full serving of café au lait. "I didn't want to worry you."

"Feed that line to someone else, child. Mothers have a God-given right to worry. Don't you go thinking yourself too grand to deny me my rights."

Serena slid into the seat beside her mother and shoveled two teaspoons of unrefined sugar into her drink. "You had enough on your plate with Sammie moving home and Daddy cutting her off."

Endora's huff had a grunt behind it that was terribly unattractive, unlike her mother's appearance even at this early hour. She sat coiffed and coutured and ready to take on the entire spirit and human realms at seven o'clock in the morning. Her dark hair, streaked with gray in a perfect pattern to add credence to her paranormal profession, didn't have a strand out of place. Her dress, full-length with a swirl pattern that covered the complete spectrum of blues from powder to midnight, didn't have a wrinkle and draped attractively over a body only slightly larger in size than it had been when Serena was born. Her makeup, worn slightly thicker than in years past, gave her an otherworldly wisdom that Serena had seen in action on more than one occasion.

Her mother was all things most mothers were, and more: eccentric, intrusive, demanding. But she loved Serena. She'd proven that more times than Serena dared count lest her guilt overcome her.

"I'll be fine," Serena said, touching her mother's hand in a gesture meant to be soothing. "Brandon's here."

Her mother surveyed her beneath thick lashes. "I

wasn't too worried about *that* until he met me at your back door with a handgun."

Serena took a sip of coffee and pictured the scene. "And he didn't shoot? They *did* teach you restraint in the army, didn't they?"

Brandon bit back a smile. "You ain't whistlin' Dixie, sister."

Endora glared at both of them until Serena felt a pang of remorse. Her mother endured enough disrespect and doubt from naysayers who questioned her psychic gifts. Like Brandon. She didn't need such sass from her daughter.

"I'm sorry, Mother. We're just teasing you. Brandon was protecting me. He wouldn't have drawn his gun if he'd known you were coming. I thought we were going to meet at your place."

"Yes, well, I changed my mind when my phone rang at five-thirty this morning with Tillie spreading some tale about a brick through your window." She pointed a finger at Brandon. "Your aunt is a terrible gossip. Your uncle gives her what-for about that every time we talk to him."

Brandon's eyebrows slanted over disbelieving eyes. His uncle Hank had been dead for twenty-seven years.

Endora continued her rant. "But she's accurate, that I'll give her." She turned to Serena. "I'm sure this Chance boy had something to do with you not calling and telling me yourself."

Serena never had been a snitch regarding Brandon and her mother. She wasn't about to start now.

"I wasn't hurt. I didn't see any reason to wake you up and have you rush over here just to tuck me into bed."

"So you had him do it?"

Miss Lily cleared her throat as she swung the cast-iron griddle off the gas burner with more steadiness and strength than her seventy-year-old arms should have. "Where's the platter, Serena? That young man looks hungry and my arms are tired of stirring."

Serena jumped up and obediently slid a platter from a lower shelf, laughing to herself at Miss Lily's well-timed interruption. She knew Serena's kitchen better than Serena did. She just wanted to put a stop to the bickering and sniping. Good thing too, or Serena would have a headache ten times stronger than the one currently being chased away by French-roasted caffeine.

Her mother resumed an air of utter dignity, snapping a napkin onto her lap, as Serena placed the hash in the center of the table alongside a steaming basket of freshly baked buttermilk biscuits and a bowl of fruit compote. Brandon did the same with his napkin. Serena could practically hear the thrumming rumble of a snare drum in the background, keeping time for the duelers as they bowed politely before walking ten paces and firing again. The delicious aromas of Miss Lily's breakfast battled with the air of conflict in the kitchen.

"Brandon, honey." Miss Lily's voice, a musical mix of New Orleans local and old-time Southern belle, broke the tension as she folded herself into her chair. "What about those brothers of yours? Tillie's been stingy with her tales of those two, what with you comin' home and all."

Serena relaxed when she watched Brandon's scowl melt into a reluctant grin. He never could resist loving

Miss Lily as much as she did, no more than he could hide his love for his brothers. As they ate, he recounted Kellan's glorious exploits as a decorated Navy SEAL and told, with only a little concern showing through, about T.J.'s new obsession with extreme sports.

In the truest Southern tradition, they avoided discussion of the threats on Serena during the entire meal. When Serena rose with Miss Lily to start clearing the table, Brandon cleared his throat and addressed her mother pointedly.

"Endora, I want you to know I not only intend to make sure no harm comes to Serena, I plan to find out who was responsible for that brick through her window. You may not trust me much, but you have to admit that I've been keeping Serena out of trouble nearly as long as you have."

Endora folded her napkin and placed it squarely beside her. She assessed Brandon with eyes both visible and invisible—the eye of a mother and the eye of a woman guided by things others couldn't see.

"You've caused her a great deal of trouble too, Brandon Chance. And I don't think you're through yet."

Brandon held her gaze. "No, ma'am, I'm probably not. But the kind of danger I pose won't get her killed."

Standing, Endora waved at Lily, indicating she was ready to leave. "You see to that, young man. Or you'll have me to deal with."

"THAT WENT BETTER than I expected," Serena said after walking Endora and Miss Lily to the vintage Duesenburg her mother drove around town. Brandon had already started to fill her sink with water and soap and stacked the dishes to soak. He turned off the faucet when she closed the front door, and met her in the living room, the added shade of the boxed-up window reminding both of them that they had no time to waste.

"Time to talk, Serena."

"I have to let Maurice out."

"Already done. Filled his water dish, too. The breakfast plates can wait. Who has a key to this house other than your mother and Miss Lily?"

Serena shook her head, wondering who could have possibly gained entrance to her house without her knowledge and then shuffled through the papers in her casket to find the fake notes. She'd carefully hidden the notes beneath at least three years' worth of warranties, birthday cards and receipts.

"They have one key between them. Miss Lily uses it to fill my fridge. Mother rarely comes over when I'm not here—she's too busy."

"What about your sister?"

Serena concentrated, trying to remember if she'd given Sammie a key over the past month—not because she believed her sister had anything to do with the brick through the window, but because she wouldn't waylay Brandon's suspicions in any other way.

"She's only been in town a month. I'd remember if I gave her a key. I haven't."

"And you didn't tell her about your scheme to break your engagement with Drew?"

Serena shook her head and plopped onto the couch. "Sammie wouldn't have approved."

"She wants you to marry Drew?"

She couldn't contain her laugh. "Uh, no. But she's a direct-approach kind of person. When she wants something, she just goes after it until she gets it. She'd want me to do things and say things that would crush Drew. I won't do that," she said one more time for emphasis.

Brandon only shook his head.

"You've never sent David here on an errand with a key, or any of your other employees?"

For the sake of cooperation, she thought carefully about his question. Besides, she really did want to know what the heck was going on. "Not since I created the notes and shoved them in the box."

"Where did you make the notes? At the spa?"

"I'm not stupid, Brandon." She'd been extremely careful to ensure that no one found out about her plan. "I went to a copy center in Metairie, where no one knew me. I rented a computer and I didn't save the files."

He thought for a moment. "The machine could have had an automatic save feature. Someone could have stumbled onto your work after you left, maybe followed you home."

Serena wanted to deny the possibility, but her knowledge of computers was limited to the style she'd used in college, now long out of date. She knew just enough about current technology to function well in her business, maybe a little more than most people because of her friendship with Drew, who owned an Internet company. But she wasn't certain of her knowledge, that was for sure.

"I don't think so, Brandon. But I could be wrong. I'm not sure of all the features on the new operating systems, but I can't see how finding a file on a rented computer would lead someone to me. I logged in under a fake name. I chose a machine in a corner where no one could look over my shoulder."

He nodded, obviously impressed. "After you get dressed, we'll go over to Metairie. You can show me the shop and which machine you used." He slid his hands into his pockets, and for the first time this morning, Serena noticed how snug his jeans were and how very nicely he filled them out. Even his dour expression couldn't dispel her silent sigh.

"Last question, Serena. What about Drew? Does he have access to your house?"

Serena rolled her lips together, fighting not to bite the inside of her mouth. While she'd never given Drew his own copy of her back-door key, he'd used hers on hundreds of occasions—to grab her extra clothes when a customer ran late and they had an engagement after work, or to feed Maurice and Tabitha when she'd gone out of town. If memory served, he'd run such an errand for her on Saturday, when the spa was overbooked and she'd run out of fresh aloe. But despite Brandon's conjecture last night giving Drew a tentative yet plausible motive, she couldn't imagine he'd stoop to such measures to convince her to marry him.

Her uncertainty, however, must have shown on her face. Brandon ran his hands through his hair and sat beside her on the couch.

"He does have a key."

"No, but he's borrowed mine a million times." And Drew was just the type to make a copy for emergencies. And he most definitely knew that any personal paper of the slightest importance was stored in her antique casket. "Brandon, he just can't be behind this. It's not like Drew to do something as dangerous as throw-

ing a brick through my window. He could have hurt
me, or one of the animals. Tabitha could have been sitting on that sill."

"Does she usually sit there at night?"

"Cats don't have schedules, but no, she's usually in
bed with me at that time...or in the pantry. But Drew
wouldn't know that. He's never..."

Her words trailed off, but Brandon took great pleasure in filling in the rest of the sentence. *He's never
stayed here that late.* Or better still, *He's never stayed here
overnight.* Since Serena claimed not to be in love with
Drew, not to want this marriage to go forward, he'd
hoped they hadn't been intimate—not that her sex life
was any of his business.

But he'd make it his business. After last night, he
didn't have much choice. And conveniently, his investigation gave him the reason to ask.

"You and Drew haven't slept together here?"

Any other woman might have been shocked by his
forthright question. Serena just smirked.

"You've been wanting to ask that question, haven't
you?"

Suddenly, trying to convince her he was just working on a case didn't seem as plausible as it had a
moment ago.

"Since you walked into my office yesterday," he admitted. No sense in lying to her when he wanted nothing less than the whole truth in return.

She licked her lips and fluffed her hair, leaning back
into the pillows of the couch and staring up at him with
eyes weary from lack of sleep, but still sparkling with
the irony of his concern. "Drew and I haven't slept together, Brandon. Not here, not anywhere. I told you, I

don't want to marry him. I'm not a tease. When I want a man, he knows."

Brandon inhaled, then held his breath for a long moment before blowing it out through his mouth. He knew, all right. And he was in serious trouble. He watched her swivel ever so slightly and drape her arm over the overstuffed cushion beside her. Sensuality and Serena went hand in hand. Her signals were as clear as a radar blip in the center of the screen, her weapons as dangerous as AMRAAM missiles on a MiG.

In the interest of keeping her safe, he'd fight the good fight to resist her. Their make-out session on the couch had kept him awake all night. He could only imagine what making love with her would do to his ability to function.

"I've made a mental note of that, thanks." With one more fortifying breath, he stood, swiveled on his heel and marched to the kitchen. "I'll tackle the dishes. You get dressed. I want to get to the bottom of this today."

He plunged his hands into the steaming, sudsy water, not bothering to glance over his shoulder. If he knew Serena, and unfortunately he did, she was grinning from ear to ear. She'd just won a small but significant battle. She knew without a doubt that he wanted her more than he would admit.

But he wouldn't lose the war. He'd sworn to protect her—and that he would do. From her stalker. And from himself.

Especially from himself.

9

THEY DROVE BACK from Metairie in silence, no closer to figuring out who'd threatened Serena than before. After conferring with the copy-shop manager, Brandon was convinced that no one could have seen Serena's notes once she deleted the documents. Even the printer she'd used was directly beside the terminal she'd rented. Her alias had indeed shown up on the company's records, but neither the manager nor his college-age assistant recognized Serena in her normal clothes.

Though "normal," Brandon noted, was a relative statement with Serena. The night she'd made the notes, she'd reportedly worn a baggy Tulane sweatshirt, cap and jeans. He wished she'd adopt the same mode of dress every day, but instead she'd wrapped herself in another of her slenderizing sarong skirts, topped with a snug, V-necked tank top and an unbuttoned, tied-at-the-waist blouse. With gold sandals and enough rings and bracelets to stock a jewelry cart on the Square, Serena wasn't exactly a woman any red-blooded American male could miss.

And he'd never felt the simmering effects of his own red blood more than he had over the past two days.

"We've fairly eliminated a stranger from being responsible," he pointed out, trying to waylay his attraction, trying to remember that Serena could be nothing more than a client, and an old friend, but definitely not a lover.

"I can see why we might think that," she replied.

Her reluctance to see the obvious succeeded in tamping down his unbidden desire to pull off the interstate and kiss the anxiety off her face.

"Can you see why we might not? Come on, Serena. This has *inside job* written all over it." Actually, Brandon was quite certain it had *Drew Stuart* written all over it, but he wasn't the type to go accusing a man without real proof. Proof he intended to get—today.

"I want to go to the spa." Her change of subject didn't surprise him. Neither did her choice of retreats, though he wasn't sure taking her to a public place was a good idea.

"I'm not..."

"Don't say no, Brandon. The brick went through the window of my house. The spa is completely booked today. I can't leave David and the rest of my staff shorthanded, not after dropping Maurice and Tabitha II off there for safekeeping."

Serena had insisted on removing both animals from the house if they were going to be gone all day. With her mother and Miss Lily out visiting clients and Samantha's tiny new apartment pet restricted, they'd had no choice but to drop them off at the spa before heading out on their fact-finding mission. As Brandon maneuvered his Jeep off I-10, he reevaluated his initial reluctance to leave Serena at the spa. She would indeed be safe, at least for an hour or two.

And an hour or two was all he needed to find Drew and get the truth—even if he had to beat it out of him.

For some reason, the prospect of physical violence

against a guy he used to call a friend didn't rub against his grain the way it should. Brandon was a risk-taker, had been a certified daredevil in his youth, but he'd never been particularly violent. And yet, just the thought of Drew presuming some warped type of ownership over Serena made his knuckles itch to pound on flesh.

"What's your sister doing today?" he asked.

"Working if she didn't already quit. Why?"

He shrugged as he took a left onto Chartres Street. "I'd feel better if she could come by the spa and stay with you."

That perked her up. She sat up straighter in her seat and turned to face him as much as her seat belt would allow. "Really? You mean you might actually consider letting Sammie work with you?"

"Don't jump to conclusions. I still want her to do her research and get her licenses before I make a decision. But I wouldn't mind her help today—if she's really as observant as she claims and wasn't exaggerating about her black belt."

Serena leaned her cheek against the headrest. Through his peripheral vision, he caught the weariness in her body language and his insides heated with the renewed fire of anger and frustration and plain old caveman protectiveness.

"If she says she's good, I believe her," Serena responded. "She's not a braggart. She tells it like it is."

"Is that why your father cut her off?" He'd wanted to ask that question since this morning when Serena had made the cryptic statement to her mother. Devlin Deveaux's fame rivaled Steven Spielberg's, or at least Martin Scorsese's. He had money coming out of his ears. Brandon couldn't imagine why he'd withhold anything from the daughter he'd raised.

"*Cut her off* is misleading, but that's how Mother sees it."

Brandon was suddenly glad he'd asked. He liked the sound of the ire in her voice. Any fiery emotion was preferable to the quiet, fear-laden resignation he'd heard before.

"How so?" They had a few minutes until they reached the spa. He might as well get the whole story.

As expected, Serena obliged. "Samantha had her own money from working. Unfortunately, she most often worked for my father, and he preferred to pay her with interest in his movies, then talked her into reinvesting in the next one. He's over budget this time and she hasn't seen a dime since a few months before she left California. He *says* he's made her a producer and that it'll be his biggest hit yet, but since production won't be done for a while, Sammie's purse has been a little empty. She used all her savings just to move back here."

"And she doesn't want handouts from Mom or sis?"

"Not if she can help it. It's not her style."

Turning on Toulouse Street, Brandon maneuvered the Jeep down the narrow brick road, watching for a parking spot. Serena and Samantha may not have been raised in the same household, but both women were as fiercely independent as any of the guys he'd ever served with, maybe even more so. He'd be damned if he let Drew, or whoever was responsible for the brick, take that away from either one of them.

He found a spot and parked, commanding Serena to stay in the Jeep until he got out and surveyed the area.

Satisfied no one or nothing suspicious was occurring beyond the regular midmorning mayhem of the Quarter, he opened her door and helped her out. In the process, he was treated to a quick flash of thigh from the split in her skirt.

He really did have to solve this case fast.

The minute the doors of the spa jingled open, Brandon watched Serena put on her best professional face. She greeted customers waiting in the lobby with familiarity and genuine warmth, even the ones she was meeting for the first time. He remained near the door, watching David answer a string of calls with his headset while serving tea to patrons.

"Mr. Chance," David greeted after handing out the last porcelain cup and saucer. "I brewed a killer oolong this morning. Want a cup?"

Brandon shook his head and watched Serena disappear beyond the beaded drapes, her massage therapist in tow.

"I'm not staying. Do you know how to get in touch with Serena's sister?"

"Yeah, she's in Serena's office trying to keep Maurice from eating the cat." He grimaced and glanced down, drawing Brandon's attention to the pet fur coating his jeans. "They supposedly get along, but Serena once told me she'd designed the spa to bring the most basic emotions to the surface." He swiped impotently at his pants. "I'm starting to believe her."

And in that case, he really should be getting the hell out, Brandon acknowledged with a nod. "Can you ask Sam to keep an eye on her sister for me? I have an important errand."

"I think that's why she's here," David confided. A

gentle chirping indicated another call coming in, so he pressed a button hooked onto his belt loop and answered, "Serena's Spa and Scents, may I help you?" He listened for a moment, then catching the impatience on Brandon's face, he asked the caller to please hold.

"Thanks," Brandon said, liking the boy more and more by the minute. "One last thing. Do you have a business and home address for Drew Stuart?"

David's expression revealed a mix of surprise and suspicion.

"He's an old friend of mine, too. And I'd like to pay him a visit."

SERENA WANDERED INTO the garden, watching the shadows elongate as day surrendered to night. Thank God for a busy schedule. She'd been so wrapped up in her customers and their needs, she'd been completely unable to think of her own troubles for more than an instant. Invariably, even those brief thoughts were interrupted by a problem with Maurice, a call from a supplier, a joke from her sister or the message that Brandon's errands would take a little longer than he'd planned and he wouldn't be back to fetch her until closing time.

Which had come and gone. At nearly eight o'clock, the space she'd so lovingly designed for clean comfort now echoed with an emptiness she'd never before experienced. She could hear the gentle tapping of David's fingers on his keyboard out front, working on a paper for his rhetoric class here instead of at his dorm because he didn't want to leave her and Samantha alone until Brandon returned. *Men.* Though David wasn't exactly a grunt-and-bang-his-chest type, he couldn't fight his natural instincts any more than she could. And those instincts had been on superpowered overdrive all day.

Little by little, the horror and fear of the brick through her window and the copycat threat faded to the background. She'd never let fear rule her life and she wasn't about to start now.

Brandon vowed to protect her and she believed him implicitly. She didn't even worry too much over his suspicions of Drew. The more she thought about it, the more she realized how ridiculous that notion was. Though she didn't have an alternative suspect even after racking her brain as much as the day would allow, she trusted that the truth would come out soon enough.

All the truth. Particularly the truth about personal wants and needs. And she was going to be the first to start.

She'd admitted quite a bit to Brandon last night— more than she'd planned to—more than she'd known herself until she'd felt the fire in his kiss and the passion of his touch. But because Brandon was convinced he had to protect her in more ways than she'd paid for, the desire had gone unexplored. Well, she'd spent way too much spiritual energy trying to achieve simple balance in her life to let this frustration undo her. Until she and Brandon explored and dealt with everything simmering between them, finding out who'd threatened her wouldn't do much but restore an illusion of personal safety and freedom. An illusion because as long as Brandon was still in New Orleans, her heart was at risk.

So the first thing she planned to do was confront

their overwhelming, all-encompassing, hot-fire desire. He'd only kissed her a few times, yet the pressure on her lips, his taste on her tongue, still lingered, still smoldered deep inside her, ready to flare with renewed heat the minute he glanced in her direction or brushed against her skin.

Tonight, she'd sate this hunger, explore this all-too-real magic. If she didn't, she feared she'd go even more insane than Brandon already thought she was.

"Serena?" David poked his head through the beads.

Startled, Serena jumped, then tapped her chest to remind her heart to beat. "I'm out here." She stepped closer to the spa entrance. Unlike other gardens in the Quarter, hers had no street access except through the spa.

"Brandon's back," David told her. "He's helping Sam put Tabby and Maurice in her car."

Serena marched to the doors, but lingered at the threshold, not yet wanting to go inside. "She's taking them home?" *She's gonna fit Maurice into that tiny car of hers?*

David shook his head. "Your mother's home and said she'd take them until you got there. She offered your old bedroom for the night." He glanced over his shoulder, indicating to Serena that whoever was behind him wasn't too thrilled with that idea.

Brandon pushed through the beads like a bull through a red drape. "That won't be happening."

Serena grinned. She didn't want to stay with her mother. She wanted to stay with Brandon.

"Tell Sammie to promise my mother I'll call her in the morning," Serena said. "You should go home, David. Can you lock the door on your way out?"

"Sure thing." David hesitated for a moment, watching Brandon with questioning eyes, then gave up trying to decipher his unreadable expression, an expression even Serena couldn't decode. "Good night."

Neither one of them replied. They stood there staring at each other until they heard the rustle of David's backpack, the jingle of his keys and the tinkle of the front bell, followed by a click of the dead bolt.

Brandon took a single step toward her, then stopped again. She'd turned off all the lights in the spa before venturing into the garden, wanting nothing more than the glow of the stars and the Quarter to guide her pensive wandering. A sliver of light slashed across Brandon's face, throwing even more silver into the mixed hues of black and gray of his gaze and putting his mouth and jaw in shadow.

She captured her bottom lip between her teeth. "Did you find out what you wanted?"

"Not exactly."

"Wasn't Drew at his office? David told me that's who you were going to see."

"He was there."

"You don't look happy about whatever he told you."

"He didn't tell me anything I didn't already know."

Brandon clenched his fists at his sides, curling his fingers tightly, then releasing them in a stiff stretch to alleviate the sudden tension in his muscles. Drew hadn't shed any new light on Serena's troubles. Their "man-to-man" conversation did nothing more than confirm facts Brandon didn't want to face.

Like the unmistakable truth that Drew didn't love Serena, even if he thought he did. He valued her. He needed her and cared about her welfare as an old, good friend would. But his love sprang from a fear of being without her much more than from a passion he couldn't control.

And Brandon knew about that passion, knew first-hand.

He clenched his fists again.

Serena slipped away from the door and disappeared beyond his line of vision. "Do you still think he's behind the brick?"

Her voice receded. He'd have to follow her to answer, and the shadowy, intimate setting of her erotic garden wasn't the safest place for him right now...or for her.

The danger they now faced came solely from each other.

His eyes adjusted to the muted light and he spotted her walking barefoot around the back of the fountain. The water dripped and dribbled over the sensuously carved marble, providing a gentle music that offset the late-night echoes of the Quarter on the other side of the high walls.

"No, it's wasn't Drew. That couple from New York had him playing tour guide around the city until well after midnight."

"Couldn't he have hired someone?"

She played devil's advocate with a mocking lilt in her voice. She knew as well as he did now that such a nefarious plan wouldn't occur to a guy like Drew. Brandon had talked with Drew for hours. They'd reminisced, shooting the breeze until Brandon had established a comfortable rapport that led men like Drew into admitting more than they wanted to, more than they sometimes knew themselves. And while Drew had convinced Brandon that he had nothing to do with the threats on Serena's life, he'd also clued him in to the most shocking revelation of all.

"He's not the one," Brandon concluded. *He's not the one behind the threats. He's not the one who should be your husband. And he's definitely not the one to love you.*

That job's already taken.

Brandon experienced another jolt of utter disbelief at the notion that he loved Serena Deveaux, something he'd realized over a beer with Drew and had been grappling with as he wandered the Quarter considering what to do next. She most certainly wasn't the wife he'd envisioned finding when he left the service. Someone who'd cook meals and have babies and lull his restlessness into calm content when his reckless spirit threatened to take control. Someone who'd talk sense into him when he felt the urge to take to the skies in a biplane he'd rebuilt in his garage or embark on a rappelling trip to the Andes with his baby brother, T.J.

Serena wouldn't be a voice of reason to remind him he wasn't getting any younger. She wouldn't tie him down with stern looks or even sweet kisses that reminded him of his responsibilities. If Serena loved him, she'd fly the plane with him so they could make love as they soared, or she'd pack her own climbing gear so they could reach the pinnacles of sensual pleasure on one of the world's highest peaks.

If she loved him.

The possibility seemed ludicrous. Crazier than she was. Crazier than she made him. But he couldn't forget that just last night she'd kissed him with more willingness and more desire than any woman he'd ever held in his arms. He was able to forget that she had pushed him away fifteen years ago, when he was young and foolish and didn't know how to treat her right.

But he knew now. And she knew that he knew.

Her voice rolled toward him with a soft echo over the deserted garden path. "Drew's not the one for me. You are. You always have been."

His eyes caught sight of Serena in a cloak of shadows as she emerged from behind the fountain. Though they were separated by the circular pool and gurgling water, he heard her blatant feminine need—could feel the heat of her desire with the same magnetic tug that urged him to forget about his plans and his vows and do only what she was inviting him to do. The urge to resist was strong. He couldn't make promises. He couldn't change his life direction after all he'd done to lay the groundwork.

"Serena, you don't know me anymore."

"Don't fool yourself, Brandon. I know you better than you think. And I know me. I know what I want. I know what I deserve. I've always known. Always."

He watched her lift her arms behind her head and release the clasp on the bulky necklace she wore. The crafted gold dropped into the water with a gentle splash. She took off her bracelets next, laying them in a stack on the fountain's edge.

"You deserve a man who can love you forever." His platitude sounded entirely too personal, so he amended himself. "Every woman deserves that."

Her laugh was bittersweet. "Yeah, we all do. But you know what? I'll settle for a man who will love me tonight. With all his soul." She stepped over the stone edge and into the pool, her fingers working the knot on her skirt as the hem floated in the water.

"Serena..." He spoke her name to stop her, but didn't move an inch.

Her head tilted ever so slightly, just enough for her eyes to catch a gleam of starlight and reflect her intentions. "Do I need to dare you again, Brandon?"

She unwrapped the skirt, revealing her slim, bare legs and panties so pink and translucent he could see the clear outline of feminine curls as if the beam from a street lamp focused exclusively on the apex of her thighs. His groin grew tight and hot. God, he wanted her. And she most certainly wanted him. Tonight, here, would be nothing like he imagined, nothing like he'd ever planned, even when he used to fantasize about Serena beneath the covers of his bunk bed. In the flesh, willing and wanting, Serena Deveaux transcended any *Playboy*-inspired teenage dream.

Especially since he'd tasted her. Knew the abandon of her kiss, the potential freedom of her embrace.

He stepped closer as she tossed the sarong onto the ground. He kicked off his shoes when she slipped her fingers beneath the hem of her tank top, then splashed into the fountain just in front of her when she tore the shirt over her head. In a tangle of hair and bare breasts and eyes dark with desire, she revealed herself to him, offered herself, with a fundamental freedom of spirit that was hers and hers alone.

Brandon caught her elbows before she brought them down and stood, motionless, his lungs aching for something more than air, his entire body throbbing for something beyond a spontaneous seduction.

"This isn't a good idea," he said.

"Do you really want to waste time trying to convince me, which you won't...or do you just want to make love with me?"

She tugged her elbows from his grasp, threw her top aside and took his hands in hers. Turning them, she examined the breadth of his palms, the length of his fingers, the roughened texture of his skin. His legs grew heavy as his jeans saturated water from the pool. His groin thickened with long lust. How was he supposed to resist her? Here? Like this?

"You have great hands, Brandon." She met his gaze straight on—no shyness, no fear—nothing but unadulterated need and utter concentration. On him. As if he was the only man who existed in the world. As if he existed only for her.

"I asked you to touch me last night." She pressed his hands downward, skimming them down her rib cage then around her waist, allowing his fingers to brush over her skin—introducing him to her warmth with slow, directed skill. "You barely did."

The muscles in his forearms ached with paralyzing tightness. One reaction, one reflex, and he could caress her curves completely—touch her, please her, pleasure her—in every delicious way. "I wanted to touch so much more."

He'd admit that much because it was the truth. He couldn't claim that he'd resisted exploring her body last night for a good logical reason because, at this instant, he couldn't for the life of him remember what that good logical reason could possibly have been.

"But you didn't," she replied. "Because of Drew, maybe. And now you know, he has nothing to do with us. And maybe you didn't because of what happened in the past. Which is just that—in the past."

She guided his hands in a circular motion to the lowest portion of her hips, then pulled up over her abdomen, between her cleavage, over her throat and chin to her lips. She kissed each of his palms, softly, caressing her cheek against his fingers.

"What do you want now? Right now. Not tomorrow, not next week, because the future takes care of itself. I'm a 'live for the moment' kind of gal, Brandon. You know I always have been. And in this moment, living means making love with you."

He grabbed her face, held her still, searched her irises for any sign, any indication, that she'd regret her seduction in the light of the day. Because if he made love to her, he'd do so all night. To make sure she never forgot. To make sure he always remembered the night his greatest fantasy came true.

"What'll it be, Brandon? Live or run?"

He dipped his head and captured her lips, muttering the last words he intended to speak for a long while.

"Chance men *never* run."

10

FOR A KISS THAT started with a slow, deliberate tease,
the pace accelerated instantaneously the minute Brandon accepted her challenge. With one hand still on her
cheek and the other flat and hot and strong against her
lower back, he pressed her full against him and devoured her mouth. With a sigh and a thrill, Serena surrendered, released his hand and untucked his shirt.

She slid her hands upward, marveling at the rock-
hard tension in his muscles and the erotic skill of his
tongue. Her senses reeled. She didn't know what felt
better—her fingers curled with the hair on his chest or
her mouth entwined with his. He was so hard. She was
so soft. She wanted to feel him fully against her. Inside
her.

She forced him to break the kiss long enough to tear
his shirt over his head. He bent forward to take her
mouth again, but she stepped back, sloshing water
high against their knees and thighs.

She shook her head and undid his button fly. He
grabbed the marble statue for balance, his chest heav-
ing with barely checked control while she worked his
jeans and boxers off his body.

Lord, he was magnificent. She couldn't help but stop
and compare the lines of the carved stone with the living, breathing counterpart that leaned against it. She
couldn't help but run her hands first over the marble to

steal the cool moisture dribbling across the curves, then over Brandon's body—arms first, then down his back.

He turned as though to step out, but she stopped him.

"Don't move. We have all night. I just want to feel you."

His back still to her, she scooped up a handful of water and released it at his waist, then watched, fascinated, as the rivulets swirled over his backside and down his powerful legs. Then she followed the drops with her hands.

She didn't shy from touching him. He didn't shy from groaning his approval of her exploration or from seeking out her mouth, branding her with a probing kiss of his own.

"You got me all wet," he said.

She searched his eyes for humor, but found only a glimmer of amusement in the blackness of his gaze.

"Just a little damp," she answered, her lips, swollen and aching for his, curled into a tiny smile. She had to tilt her head back to look at him directly and he immediately sensed the discomfort that caused.

His hands, wet from his hold on the statue, slipped down her back with a slowness that mirrored her touch, but when he reached her backside, he cupped her and lifted her onto the fountain, sliding her full against marble, her feet poised along the lower edge. Her curves nearly fit with complete perfection, as if she'd let the artist mold the stone against her naked body.

"Now I know why this fountain is so erotic," he murmured, looking down to how the tiny seat in the stone spread her legs just so wide. "It's shaped for a woman." His gaze met hers. "For you."

"I'm sure it's a coincidence," she insisted, but heat pooled between her legs as he lifted her right arm and draped it over a jutted curve, then did the same to her left, leaving her like an open offering to him.

Which she was. In every single aspect of her being, fountain or not.

"I don't believe in coincidences."

"What do you believe in, Brandon?" She couldn't help ask because she really didn't know. Minutes ago, she didn't care, but now, she was vulnerable to him. To his touch and his control over the desire throbbing through her veins and over skin like a pulsing, living heat.

He leaned forward and kissed her temple. "I believe in knowing every inch of you, *chére*. I believe in soft kisses and wet tongues and hard nipples and hot centers and loud orgasms. Really loud ones. Ones where you shout my name so the whole Quarter can hear."

She didn't know if she had wanted a more soulful answer when she first asked, but the one he provided suited her just fine. He ran his tongue to her ear, teasing her flesh with hard moisture and heated breath, nibbling her lobe while his hands hovered beside her cheeks.

"I've waited a lifetime to touch you, Serena."

"Don't wait," was all she could manage, her lungs tight with anticipation. She'd waited that same lifetime to be touched by him, to join with him, the only man she'd ever loved.

"I won't. Now don't move."

He delayed no longer, but he didn't use his hands to

explore her. First, he used his eyes, followed by his mouth and tongue. He kissed a path down the column of her neck, across her shoulders and over one arm, then back to the base of her neck. He stepped back and quickly assessed her position.

"Here," he said, grasping her chin and tilting it just a smidgen to the left.

When he did, a splash of running water crossed over her shoulder and down her breast. Her sharp intake of breath thrust the nipple forward and he wasted no time capturing it in his mouth, lapping the water as he covered her sensitive flesh with his warm mouth.

Serena pressed her lids closed. The sensation made her eyes hot with tears, hot with blinding need. He sucked and teased and laved and kissed with a pace just quick enough to make her relish every sensation—and just slow enough to mourn the loss of his mouth when he slid down to his knees and braced his hands along the outside of her thighs.

The fountain's water bubbled beneath her, ran down her back with cool caresses, contrasting with Brandon's hot hands skimming over her legs. His fingers teased. His eyes feasted. Serena held her breath, praying he'd taste her soon, before she lost her ability to speak.

He started at her knees and nibbled his way up. He took a deep breath, then blew hot warmth across her curls. When he finally tasted her, she swallowed a desperate cry. It wasn't enough. Delicious and delectable as his rigid tongue felt against her swollen, pounding flesh, she wanted more.

"Brandon." She spoke his name in yearning, unhooking her arms from the marble to raise his head.

He looked up with eyes darker than a bayou sky. "I said, don't move," he chastised, lust and devilish intentions curving his mouth into a mock frown. "Can't you ever listen?"

"But..." Her protest died a pleasurable death when he wrapped his full mouth against her and flicked her words out of her mind. She was his. For now, all his.

And she told him so. Loudly.

When he finally stood and kissed away the last vestiges of her climax, she regained her ability to think. Soon, very soon, they were going to make love. And they'd need protection.

"There's a box of condoms in my office." She whispered the fact against his lips, praying she wouldn't destroy the magical mood.

"I was going to ask you about that." His voice brimmed with gentle teasing. He'd obviously somehow found time in the past two days to rummage through her things. "Is there something you need to tell me about the massages you give at this place?"

She laughed because she knew he was baiting her, teasing her. Because that's what they did, she and Brandon. For as long as they'd known each other.

But the amiable ribbing took on a delicious naughtiness now, making her nipples tighten and her heart flutter when he gave her a playful wink.

"Why tell when I'm having so much fun showing you?" she answered.

"Good point. I'll be right back. Don't move."

She waited until he splashed out of the fountain before she slid down the marble and into the water, cooling her hot flesh against the mosaic tiles. She tried not to think about the consequences of what they'd just done, of what they were going to do. She'd allowed Brandon access to so much more than just her body. She'd pay a steep price for her sensual candor.

But as she leaned back on her elbows, submerging her flaming skin in the fountain's cool waters, she knew she'd have no regrets. Not with Brandon. She no longer lamented the years they'd lost since that night in the gym, the friendship they'd sacrificed. She now saw it all clearly as a path to precisely this spot. This moment.

This ecstasy.

He was in and out of her office in record time. He ripped a condom out of the box, tore the foil packet with his teeth, tossed it onto the edge of the fountain and joined her in the water, crawling over her but holding his body rigid and aloft as if he was about to start a repetition of push-ups.

"You moved," he protested.

"I plan on moving a lot in the next few hours. I'm not a passive lover, Brandon. At least, I don't think I am."

"Don't think? You've done this before, right?"

She grinned, certain she wasn't going to tell him one single secret about her sex life. "Not here." She leaned up and kissed a corner of his chin. "Not like this. Not with you."

"Your first time should have been with me." He let out that feral growl of his and pressed his lips to her temple, then down her cheek.

She managed only a breathy "yeah," before he covered her mouth with his. She grabbed his marble-hard biceps, noting the restraint he used to keep from drowning her in either the water or the fullness of his desire. She knew Brandon. She knew when he was holding back. And he now had an industrial-strength wall of restraint in place, keeping him in check. In line. Unlike the way he'd been all those years ago.

Unlike the way she wanted him to be right now.

"Come here," she said. She scooted back on her elbows, wickedly tracing his body with her toes as she slipped away.

He cleared his throat before he asked, "Where?"

Pushing back with his arms, he allowed her room to slither away like a sensual sea creature of ancient myth. She rolled onto her belly, treating him to a tantalizing glimpse of her pale, bare bottom before she disappeared behind the fountain. He didn't think he could grow any harder, but he was wrong. His hands ached to hold her close, to spread his tanned fingers and roughened palms over her incredible curves, to bury himself inside her and let loose the fullness of his desire.

Serena was all that was feminine, but he'd never call her delicate. She possessed a strength that was physical and spiritual and sensual all at the same time.

And yet, he wondered if even she could match the raging need tearing through him. He'd never realized how strong his passion for her was, how intense. Though she moved away from him, an invisible connection much like a steel towline cranked a painful tension between his heart and hers.

He heard her stand, saw the droplets of water splashing as she climbed the back side of the marble.

"If you thought that side of the marble was interesting—" she noted.

First, he saw one calf, then the other, and just above, an ivory swell of flesh beckoned him like a golden light leading him home. He sloshed gallons of water over the sides of the fountain when he retrieved the condom and cursed the wetness while he forced the latex on.

But force he did.

She leaned on a small, tilted tableau just perfectly shaped and angled to support her belly and rib cage, then curved along the top to caress her breasts with cold, wet marble.

"Look what I found," she said.

He eased up behind her, emboldened by her sharp intake of breath when he pressed his full sex against her derriere. She stretched her hands behind her and grabbed his hips.

"You still think the artist didn't design this fountain for lovemaking?" he asked.

Thigh to thigh, he slipped his feet between hers, easing her legs apart while he bathed the back of her neck in kisses.

"Think?" She rolled her head forward and grabbed him tighter, pulling him so close, he had no choice but to slip between her legs to meet her demand. "Who can think?"

She leaned completely against the tableau, nestling herself so close to him, Brandon knew the minute he could no longer operate on logic or reason or thought. Instinct—primal and ingrained into all of him that was male—overtook him in a rush of pure need. He wanted to drive himself inside. Take her. Brand her.

But her coo, soft and feminine and lilting with pleasure, gripped his heart and led him inside more slowly. He relished the feel of her warmth surrounding him. Wet. Welcoming. Like velvet. Like silk.

He explored her with his hands while he strummed

a gentle rhythm. Her breasts were warm and heavy. She encouraged his touch with a litany of words. *Yes. Touch me. Brandon.*

Some words were more erotic.

Some were unintelligible, but it didn't matter. Just the sound of her voice, coming from the place deep inside her, where he needed to be, guided him, urged him.

She relaxed her shoulders and swayed her hips, rocking him deeper, sealing him to her, proving she wanted all that he could give. And yet, when he came, he wanted to look into her eyes and watch the precise moment when she took all he had in his soul.

Leaning full against her, he slipped both arms around her waist lifted her off the tableau. He loved her breasts with his hands while he backed them up to the edge of the water, then adored her nipples, neck and mouth with his lips and tongue as he turned her around, sat down and guided her onto his lap, pressing back into her tight warmth.

She didn't speak. She only smiled, folded her legs around his waist and her arms around his neck, pulled herself up and then back down to restart their elemental rhythm.

She never closed her eyes. His peripheral vision blurred as they rocked, but he found a steady center in her sea-green gaze, discovered the full breadth of Serena's power as they pumped toward the edge...then spilled over, drop by drop, jet by jet, into a sparkling pool of release.

SERENA FOLDED the fluffy terry-cloth robe around her as she puttered around inside the spa, warding off the

chill of Brandon's departure. He'd only gone back to
the garden to retrieve the box of condoms, and yet she
felt his absence with an emptiness she had no business
feeling. Tonight wasn't about happily-ever-afters or
marriage proposals or houses on Lake Pontchartrain
complete with green lawn, carport and whitewashed
fence.

But as she poured hot, freshly brewed tea into two
porcelain cups and inhaled the relaxing aroma of
chamomile and the sense-enhancing aspects of cloves,
she knew tonight hadn't been about just mindless sex
or unrequited lust.

She and Brandon had made love like two souls
joined by more than passion. More than trust. More
than love, if that was possible.

But now that she'd had Brandon inside her, she honestly considered believing that anything was possible,
anything at all—including a future for them. Together.

Until this moment, she'd never really allowed herself to think about the future beyond the next day.
She'd never dreamed about the perfect husband or
imagined becoming a mother or wife. Her devotion to
simplicity required she put her faith in making the
most of the day at hand and letting the future take care
of itself.

But if Brandon was the future's idea of her ideal
mate, she wondered if her faith had been incredibly
well placed or inherently misguided.

Brandon had once been a loyal friend. Now he was
the most magnificent lover. But he still held back a part
of himself from her—an integral part, the driving force
of who he was deep down. Even in the years of their
childhood friendship, he'd never allowed her that

close. Pride and bravado and good humor had always waylaid her, tricked her into believing she knew more about him than she actually did.

Even now, when she felt certain she knew him better than any other woman ever had, she didn't fool herself.

Brandon Chance was still a mystery—one he guarded with more vigilance than he'd ever use to protect a client. Even her. And she wasn't entirely sure she knew how to solve the complete puzzle. Or if she wanted to.

She drizzled some honey into her cup and stirred her tea, aware of the exact moment Brandon entered the spa behind her. She'd spread a blanket of towels over the carpeted area in the center and lit rows of candles along the walls.

During the day, this was a soothing but efficient place of business. But in the shadows of the Quarter, when the antique clock in her office chimed the three o'clock hour and Brandon filled the room with his heat, the space became a personal, erotic haven filled with possibilities that undid the soothing effects of even her strongest herbs.

"David said you didn't like tea," she said, slipping her fingers beneath the saucers and lifting, "but I don't have much else to offer you."

Turning, she started at the sight of him, naked and glorious and grinning like a thick-maned lion sated by the meat of a fresh kill.

"You've offered me everything I could ever want, Serena."

A shy grin bubbled to her lips before she could call it back or mold it into a smile more beguiling or seductive. Even in the afterglow of orgasms that had indeed echoed right over the marble stones of her garden wall, he could still evoke that part of her that remained a precocious child.

He accepted the tea and then followed her when she sat on the towels.

"Does that mean you're done wanting me?" She tried to inject her voice with playful seduction, but his expression hardened and the corners of his lips tilted downward in a deep frown.

"I'll never be done wanting you, Serena. Never. But that doesn't mean..."

"That we can have anything beyond tonight. I know. Well—" she wrapped her palm around her cup and slid the saucer away "—I know that you believe we can't have anything beyond tonight. And I respect that."

"But you don't understand it." He set the tea on the floor and then moved behind her and sat, drawing her between his legs so that her head rested against the crook of his shoulder and her back pressed into his chest with natural ease.

"Your logic was always beyond me, Brandon."

His chuckle warmed her insides before her swallow of tea slid down her throat. "I don't think that's the case, Serena. My logic is too simple for your complex thought patterns. You're way beyond me, sweetheart."

"You really think I'm smart?"

"I think you're brilliant. Wacky and quirky and nuts most of the time, but other than your insistence on subjecting yourself to me, I think you're damn remarkable."

"What's so wrong with subjecting myself to you?" She snuggled closer to him, reveling in the feel of his hard warmth and the mixed scents of sated passion, brewed herbs and sweet honey.

He slid his arms around her and buried his face in her hair, which had dried in haphazard ringlets that undoubtedly resembled a kitchen mop.

"Nothing is wrong, absolutely nothing. I've missed you, Serena. There were so many times I wanted to call or write, stop pretending that you'd done more than just put me in my place as you had every right to."

"Then why didn't you?"

Brandon smiled and inhaled before he answered, loving the heady smell that was hers and hers alone. She simply didn't understand the concept of guarding her thoughts or reining in her emotions. Serena operated on a level above and beyond most everyone he knew. When she wanted, she figured out a way to get. When she didn't want, she denied. He'd seen both sides of her.

He most definitely liked the wanting-taking side better.

"We're not good for each other," he answered.

She snorted in a decidedly unfeminine way. "Excuse me? You expect me to believe that after..." She waved her hand toward the garden and he knew precisely what she meant.

Their lovemaking had been incredible, the stuff of erotic fantasy and undeniable trust and exploration. They'd utilized each and every curve of the statue at the center of the fountain—more than once—and wondered if the sculptor had been an absolute genius or a complete deviant. They'd run through the garden nude and unfettered, like children unleashed on Eden, then coupled on the soft grass like lovers with eternity at their disposal.

But they didn't have eternity. They had only tonight. And Brandon had to make sure Serena understood, before he did something despicable like break her heart.

"I didn't mean we're not good for each other *that* way. I've never made love with a woman like I have with you, Serena."

"But..."

Because he couldn't help himself, he undid the tie on her robe and slipped his hands inside, skimming her satin skin with hungry hands.

"But beyond lovemaking and double dares, we're trouble together. This may sound really dull to someone like you, but I need to find a woman who will rein me in, keep me in line."

"You want to marry a drill sergeant?"

She laughed, but her comment, fraught with sarcasm, couldn't be ignored. He flattened his hands against her stomach and took a deep breath.

"If you'd met my drill sergeant, you wouldn't joke about that," he answered, suddenly uncertain if Serena really was totally wrong for him. He'd pondered the question for years, made his decision and focused on it for so long. Considering another path now seemed foolish, childish, as if he was allowing his hormones to influence his actions. He'd done that once too and had hurt her horribly.

"I'm not joking," she said, running her fingernails over his knuckles. "You have this plan for your future, a plan that doesn't include me. I'll deal with that, but I'd like to know everything you want. I never plan for the future. Life is more interesting when things just happen."

"Like tonight?"

She snuggled against him again, slid her hands completely over his and restarted his exploration by guiding him down to her lap. "Exactly like tonight."

"You don't think about what kind of man would make your life more complete?"

For a brief instant, her hands stilled and her back stiffened, as if a chill ran up her spine before she shook it away. "Tell me what you think I need, Brandon. What you think *you* need."

He closed his eyes. "We each need someone who will balance us. Keep us in line. Keep us out of trouble. Serena…"

I love you, but…

He swallowed the sentiment. He wouldn't say those words just to contradict them. They could have this night together. They could even have a friendship if she wanted to in the light of the next day. But that's all he could promise with any certainty of remaining true to his word.

"You're like a match to my wick," he said.

She nuzzled her backside against him. "I like your wick."

"Serena!"

She laughed and turned, draping herself across his lap, her eyes alight with naughtiness and insatiable intentions. Any seriousness he'd heard in her voice before was now nowhere to be seen.

"What? I do."

With unabashed candor, she wrapped her palm

around his sex and stroked with unhurried care, scooting so she could lay her cheek against his thigh.

"Serena..." As she massaged him, logic and reason and plain old common sense began drifting away. He shook his head, willing himself to hold on more tightly to his train of thought. He needed her to understand.

But how could he, when all his arguments melted away at her heated ministrations?

He opened his mouth to speak, but she rolled and kissed a trail up his inner thigh, shedding her robe as she moved.

"I know what you mean, Brandon. Tonight is about tonight. So unless you're going to use that mouth for something other than talking," she warned between nips of her teeth and soothing swipes with her tongue, "I'd keep those lips closed."

When she took him in her mouth, he leaned back in the soft towels, slid her atop him and considered only the most pleasurable uses for each and every part of his anatomy.

11

SERENA WINCED as she lifted her feet from the cobbled tiles dotting her mother's garden patio to the wrought-iron chair across from her. When her ankles sank into the downy cushions, she sighed, relishing the pleasant ache in her muscles. The memories of exactly why she felt so sore renewed the heated tingle that had haunted her all morning. She and Brandon had, in her opinion, reinvented the art of lovemaking.

They could write a scintillating addendum to the *Kama Sutra.* She imagined the accompanying illustrations while she sipped her mug of café au lait. She hadn't added enough sugar. She didn't care. She'd had enough sweetness the night before to last a lifetime.

"You look *too* happy." Samantha emerged from the house with a basket of muffins in one hand, coffee in the other and a suspicious, narrow-eyed grin curving her lips. Her hair, still streaked with blond strands from the California sun, was pulled back in a loose ponytail. Sweat-curled ringlets formed around her scrubbed-clean face and along the underside of her long neck, telling Serena she'd recently returned from her workout.

"Is there such a thing as too happy?" Serena pondered, knowing full well that her glee would be short-lived. Brandon had dropped her off at her mother's house just after sunrise, without a single promise that he'd somehow try and find a way to fit her into his carefully laid, I-just-got-out-of-the-military plans for the rest of his life.

Instead, he'd kissed her and agreed only to retrieve her no later than noon. She couldn't blame him. He'd tried to be honest with her, tried to tell her why he couldn't love her the way he should, and she'd seduced the words away. She hadn't wanted to hear his reasoning again, about fire and wicks and bad influences and the need for balance.

She was too afraid he was entirely right.

Sammie knocked Serena's legs off the other chair and sat down, bursting what was left of Serena's bliss.

"Too happy is usually a symptom of delusional behavior," Sammie noted. "Saw it all the time in Hollywood."

"Well, since most people already think I'm delusional," Serena pointed out, taking a brief sip of her chicory-and-milk brew and then fishing a hot corn muffin from the basket Sammie had laid on the table, "I'm going to enjoy being too happy. Today, anyway."

"Yeah, well, enjoy it while you can. Mother just returned from her morning consultation with the senator and she's going to make a beeline out here to find out where you've been all night, what's going on with the threats and why Brandon, your supposed bodyguard, left you unattended all morning."

That he'd been willing to part with her had surprised her a bit. She did very little arguing with him this time, only pointing out that Sammie would be over at first light and her bedroom at her mother's house was on the third floor, well out of harm's way. Besides the fact that Brandon undoubtedly remembered that

Miss Lily kept a hidden baseball bat in nearly every room and that her son, Franklin, was the six-foot-six caretaker of the property, she couldn't imagine why he'd finally heeded her pleas to suspend his body-guard duties, even for a short while.

Except that he *needed* to get away...from her.

She twisted her lips in a tight grimace as she thought, causing Sammie to shake her head.

"Too happy doesn't last long, does it?"

Serena bit into a muffin, silenced at first by the sweet buttery taste of Miss Lily's secret recipe.

"Ask me after you've eaten a muffin."

Sammie broke a steaming, golden cake in half, then popped a quarter in her mouth. She groaned with sat-isfaction, reminding Serena how she herself had made similar sounds last night—from tasting things that made even Miss Lily's muffins seem like prepackaged, convenience-store fare.

Her smile faded. She and Brandon had shared an ex-perience beyond anything she'd ever, ever imagined. They'd learned things about each other—things phys-ical, psychological, even spiritual. But the knowledge hadn't been enough to make him stay, to convince him to toss his investigation aside and carry her off to some secret hideaway where they could be alone and forget, for one more day, that someone had thrown a brick and a copycat threat through her window. She'd made the suggestion as they dressed, but Brandon had re-fused, insisting he had to find out who was threatening her as soon as possible.

And while Serena couldn't deny that his diligence and determination were part and parcel of him, she also couldn't deny that as soon as her stalker was caught, Brandon would leave her. For good.

Because she couldn't be the kind of woman he thought he needed.

Serena shook her head, forcing herself not to think about all the reasons Brandon had given her during the course of the night why their relationship could only be short-lived. He was entirely right that she acted like kerosene on his fire, and he did the same to her. They couldn't help themselves. Couldn't change who they were or the chemistry that had bound them since the moment they met. They'd proven their combustibility on the floor of the spa and then in several other locations, including the roof of her building where anyone and everyone could have spotted them had the night provided just a little more light.

Together, they tempted fate, they pushed limits, denied boundaries.

But the thrill couldn't last.

She understood better than anyone that Brandon desired and deserved stability in his life. His parents, notorious gamblers, showered their children with love, but during more than one stretch of time, they left Brandon and Kell to fend for themselves while they played the ponies in Vegas or hiked the Himalayas with T.J. in tow. They'd encouraged equally risky behavior in all their boys, buying them the toys they needed: airboats for the bayou, motorcycles to cruise the Quarter and beyond, rappelling equipment and airline tickets to the world's deepest caves and highest peaks.

If not for Aunt Tillie and her devotion to the three brothers, Serena wondered how Brandon, Kell and T.J.

would have remained alive all these years. Risking it all—gambling for the big payoff—was second nature to a Chance man.

But Brandon seemed tired of immersing himself in that lifestyle. She'd been clued in to that weariness since she'd first stepped into his office. He'd left the military behind, even though he'd loved the service. He'd chosen a new line of work that was admittedly dangerous, but he'd come home to set up shop in the one area of the world where he'd grown up feeling safe and comfortable.

While he might tempt danger during the day as a bodyguard, when he went home, he wanted to know that his wife and x-number of kids were waiting for him at the dinner table—not off concocting a new tea blend or parked in Jackson Square trading stories with the street musicians until well after midnight. He needed someone who would ease and settle his wandering, reckless ways—give him what he deserved, what he'd been denied his entire life.

Serena, unfortunately, did not have a calming effect on people. And after last night, she most definitely knew she didn't have that effect on him.

"Earth to Serena."

Serena snapped herself out of her thoughts, which had grown more and more depressing—and more and more clear—as she mused.

"I'm sorry. I didn't get much sleep last night."

Sammie's smile was pure sin and envy. "I gathered. Care to talk about it? I don't mean the details, mind you," she clarified, "but that happiness sure beat a quick path to the door."

"Yeah. Just like Brandon will as soon as he figures out who threatened me."

"What makes you so sure? Sparks fly between the two of you. It's sickening," Sammie added, never allowing her cynical nature to hide for long, "but it's special. Even Brandon is smart enough to know that."

Serena ran her fingers through her hair, curving the haphazard strands around the back of her ears. "Brandon is also smart enough to know that we're not good for each other. We never have been."

"He dumped you?"

Samantha was halfway to standing, undoubtedly ready to go beat some sense into Brandon herself, when Serena grabbed her hand and pulled her down. "No! I mean, not yet. Look, Sammie, Brandon and I are great as friends. We make life interesting for each other. We spark each other's flame, so to speak."

"Sounds like a perfect recipe for lovers," Sammie answered.

"Yeah, it does." Serena allowed herself a moment to be wistful, to remember the fire they'd stoked last night, to imagine the conflagrations they could ignite if only given the chance. But Serena had to come to grips with the fact that such a blaze more than likely wouldn't burn again. "But Brandon...and I...both want to find someone who's more than a great lover."

Until this morning, Serena never really thought about what she wanted. Little by little, the idea of marriage wasn't so bad anymore, provided she found the right person. Someone exciting. Unpredictable. Someone who might think she was crazy, but didn't mind so much. Someone strong and handsome and...

She groaned. She wanted Brandon, the one man she couldn't have.

"This is just an affair," she continued. "It'll end. Soon. As soon as his job is over. And that's okay."

Serena tossed in that last line just to see how it sounded rolling off her tongue. She sipped her coffee, but even the bitterness of the chicory didn't offset the bad taste in her mouth. Samantha watched her over the rim of her own cup, assessing her sister with her incredibly alert gaze.

Surprisingly, she didn't press further. She frowned, shook her head, then set down her cup and folded her hands on the table. "So, what's going on with the investigation? Any leads on your brick-thrower?"

The air in the garden seemed to lighten, and Serena briefly considered the irony that discussing the threats on her life was more comfortable than talking about her affair with Brandon.

"Brandon's eliminated Drew as a suspect," she answered.

Sammie snorted, then popped more muffin in her mouth. "About time. He didn't really think Drew would be that clever?"

"Clever?" Serena sat up straighter, intrigued by her sister's choice of words. "How would threatening me make him clever?"

Sammie waved her hand while she chewed and swallowed. "You know, he threatens you so you'll feel scared and then marry him to be protected. Classic woman-in-jeopardy plot."

"That's ridiculous. I'm not the 'run to my man when I'm in danger' type."

"You've never been in danger before. Who'd know

how you'd react? It might have been a decent plan, if Brandon hadn't come back to town."

"But he did, didn't he?"

Drew's voice echoed over the tiles, despite his usual soft and even volume. He stood just inside the gate, then swung the iron hinges closed behind him.

Sammie forced a swallow and picked up her coffee. "Now there's an exit cue if ever I heard one. I'll be just inside, sis."

Serena nodded, but didn't watch her sister leave. She was too shattered by the resigned expression on Drew's face. Resigned and sad. She pushed her own drink away, and the corn muffin she'd devoured suddenly felt like a stone weight in the pit of her stomach.

She scooted her chair out to stand, but he stopped her with a flattened palm.

"Don't get up. Serena, we need to talk."

He joined her at the table and sat motionless for a moment, looking at her hand as if he wanted to take it in his. She realized then that only a few days ago, he would have wrapped his fingers around hers while they spoke, without hesitating, without thinking first.

And she would have accepted that intimacy without a second thought. They were friends. Best friends. She couldn't understand why he ever wanted anything more from her. She had always been certain she'd never done anything or said anything to give him the notion she might entertain, even for an instant, the prospect of becoming his wife.

"Drew, I'm..."

"Don't apologize. I've made a royal ass out of myself over the past year, Serena. I don't know what I could have been thinking."

She shook her head as she spoke. "Just that you care about me. Just that you want to be happy. You want me to be happy."

He looked long at his lap. "It was more than that." When he met her gaze, the sorrow lingering in his blue eyes pushed the stone in her stomach up to the back of her throat. "I knew he'd come back."

"What? Who? Brandon?"

"Tillie didn't just share her gossip with your mother. She seemed to take particular pleasure in torturing me." He grinned when he spoke, acknowledging his exaggeration. "A while back, she made a comment to me that Brandon had been inquiring about office space in the Quarter. She asked me to recommend a reputable commercial real estate agent."

"When?"

"About a week before I booked the church."

Serena sighed as her heart broke and the craziness that had ruled her life over the past ten months finally made sense. "So all this 'you have to marry me whether you like it or not' was about Brandon coming back to town?"

"Can you blame me? You've been pining for him for fifteen years."

She sat up straighter and thrust her hands on her hips. "I don't *pine!*" Lord, had she been that obvious? First, her sister, who'd just moved back to town, and now the man she spent most of her free time with. They couldn't both be wrong.

"Okay, *pine* is a bad word choice," Drew admitted. "Other women pine. You ignore. You escape to this little world that exists only in your mind where you could care less about Brandon Chance or what happened the night he shattered your illusions of him. You dated. You socialized. But you never got involved with anyone. You never risked your heart."

"So what? I'm picky. Heck, I didn't want to marry you, and you're fairly perfect."

Drew impaled her with a look so brimming with common sense and pure practicality that even she couldn't deny that what he implied was true. And she knew it. She'd admitted as much to Brandon the night before.

"Okay, I *pined*," she admitted. "Sue me."

He did take her hand then and the warmth that enveloped her skin flushed straight to her heart.

"I'm not going to sue you. But I am going to bow out. I don't want to break your heart or anything," he said, all serious and yet incredibly sheepish, "but the engagement is off."

Serena exhaled, then inhaled, empowered by the scent of baked goods, coffee and magnolia...until she glanced up at the window to her mother's room. "Are you telling Endora or am I?"

"I already told her," Drew assured. "I think she's upstairs in her workshop mixing up a potion or casting a spell."

"She's a psychic, not a witch—you know that," Serena reassured him. "Now, if she calls Cousin Theodora, you're in really big trouble."

He laughed, then pulled her into his lap and gave her a brotherly hug. Serena enjoyed the sensation, knowing at once that she and Drew could finally regain the friendship his marriage quest had nearly destroyed.

"Who said the spell was for me? Endora always liked me. Brandon Chance is another story altogether."

Serena kissed Drew on the forehead and then returned to her chair. "Brandon Chance is another planet altogether. But she doesn't have to worry. After Brandon finds out who's threatened me, he'll be out my life again."

Drew's features twisted into a perplexed question mark. "Come again? You mean I'm stepping aside so you'll be alone?"

"No, you're stepping aside so we can stay friends. Brandon doesn't want someone like me in his life. Not for the long haul."

Drew shook his head. "You keep talking like that, and I'm going to start agreeing with everyone who thinks you're crazy. I saw you and Brandon together at the restaurant. I had a beer with the man yesterday. You haunt him, Serena. You always have."

Serena swiped muffin crumbs off the table and scattered them into the nearby bushes. "Except for the people my mother hangs with, haunting is not a good thing. I can't deny that we're incredibly attracted to one another, but I'm not what he needs or wants in his life. He wants someone to settle him down. Keep him home and content and happy. Someone who cooks and cleans and, I don't know, knits doilies."

When even conservative Drew blanched at the mental picture she painted, Serena wondered if Brandon had any idea what he was asking for. She couldn't imagine a man like him satisfied with a life that was predictable or stable to the point of being typical or average.

But still, it was his dream.

Who was she to burst his bubble?

"What about you? What do you want?"

Serena folded her hands in her lap. She and Drew hadn't had such an intimate conversation since college, when they'd escape to the Blacksmith's Shoppe on Bourbon Street and drink voodoo margaritas and talk about life. And as much as she wanted to share her heart with him and renew that friendship all over, she no longer knew the object of her heart's desire.

She'd wanted Brandon, heart and soul. Last night, she'd had him, and the connection was every bit as overwhelming and passionate and fulfilling as she'd imagined it would be.

But it couldn't last. Not if he truly deserved the happiness he sought, a happiness she couldn't give.

For the first time since she met Brandon on the playground, Serena honestly no longer knew what her future held, or even what she wanted it to hold.

"I want to find out who sent me that threat and have them arrested. I want to return to going where I want to go when I want to go, to not looking over my shoulder or having to drive everywhere when walking is quicker. I want to stop assessing all my customers and friends as potential criminals. I want to be free again."

Free from the threats. Free from the fear.

Free from Brandon Chance and a relationship that could never last.

BRANDON HUNG UP the phone, tapped his folders into a neat and orderly pile and stared at the clock. Just before noon. According to Samantha, Serena had been dutifully waiting for him to return and plot their next move. He assumed she was talking about the stalker.

He should have been thinking only about the stalker, about discovering the nut's identity, about fixing the situation so Serena could go about her business and live her life without him and his stupid, impossible needs.

But they were his needs, damn it. His dream. No matter how incredible Serena made him feel, no matter how extraordinary their lovemaking had been, he couldn't let go of the life he so desperately wanted. The wife and home and hearth. The average, typical, comforting family. All the things he'd missed growing up.

When the phone rang, he took a minute to script his greeting. He'd only been in business for three days.

"No Chances Protection. May I help you?"

"Brandon? Honey, is that you?"

"Mom?"

The line crackled with static and an annoying echo that told him Lynn Chance was either out of the country or using a cheap cell phone. Depending on his parents' current run of luck, he was never sure which.

"I'm in Florida."

Cheap cell phone. Monte Carlo must have been a bust.

Once his inner sarcasm subsided, he realized there would only be one reason his parents would be in Florida.

"Where's Kell?"

Kellan, a Navy SEAL, was assigned to MacDill Airforce Base in Tampa. Brandon hadn't spoken to his brother in over a month, but with him leaving on covert missions or training exercises, lack of contact wasn't unusual. His parents traveling to the Sunshine State when jai alai and greyhound racing weren't in season—that was unheard of.

"He's okay. He's in the hospital, but the doctors say he'll recover completely."

While his mother prattled on about the details, all of which meant little to Brandon so long as he'd still have his brother in one piece and functional at the end of the recovery process, Brandon swallowed a knot of regret. They'd been meaning to get together. They met up in Orlando once while Brandon trained in Miami, but that was no substitute for a real relationship.

Just like your affair with Serena, his conscience whispered.

No substitute for a real relationship.

"Can I see him if I come?" Brandon asked.

His mother paused, then asked a nearby doctor about visitors. "He'll be up and around in a few days, but you know your brother. He's mad as hell that we came. He forgets that he was once a helpless baby and that I used to bandage his scrapes, not to mention diaper his butt."

Which effectively meant that Kellan didn't like anyone seeing him so prone and vulnerable. That, Brandon could understand.

"Tell him I love him," Brandon said, "and that I'll be there if he needs me."

"He won't need you, Brandon. Your brother likes to think he doesn't need anyone. But I'm sure he'd like to see you as soon as he's up and about. Can you track down T.J.? Your father and I have no idea where he is. We've tried to leave messages on his cell phone, but he's in the mountains..."

Brandon jotted down their number, and before hanging up promised he'd find his youngest brother, who last he heard, had taken a job as an extreme-sports guide at a resort in Idaho. He knew he had the name of the place back at his apartment. And so long as Kell wasn't in any danger of death, he saw no reason to use his mother's request as an excuse to avoid collecting Serena and dealing with all that had happened between them.

On his way back to the Garden District, he reviewed what he knew about Serena's case—which wasn't much since his initial suspicion of Drew was completely off base. Whoever had thrown that brick had to have access to Serena's house to find the fake threats and then copy them. And they had to have a motive to want to harm her.

The motive threw him. Except for some sick obsession, the stalker couldn't have any real reason to hurt a gentle, free spirit like Serena. It was time to start focusing on strangers. Though Serena's antique lock on her front door was hard to open with a key, there was no telling what a talented locksmith or criminal could do with the modern lock in the back.

As soon as he collected Serena from her mother's house, he was going to begin a serious interrogation. Take her through a typical day—if she ever in her life experienced one—step by step and person by person until they came up with a new suspect. He grabbed the computer printout David had made him of spa clients and, by referring to a copy of her appointment book, he would focus on the patrons who frequented her business a little more than necessary. There had to be something he was missing, something that would lead him in the right direction to ensuring her safety.

If only he could find some way to guarantee she'd be safe from him, but his gut instinct told him that no matter how unhappy they might eventually make each other, he wasn't going to be able to let her go.

12

"SHE'S NOT OUT HERE."

Brandon's heartbeat raged in his ears. He swallowed the lump that had lodged in his esophagus, so his next words came out in a rasp. "Serena's not in the garden," he repeated.

Samantha looked up from her copy of *Bodyguard* magazine unfazed, the arches of her bare feet casually perched on the marble-topped coffee table. "What do you mean she's not there?"

"Damn it, Sam. She's not outside!"

Annoyed, Samantha slapped the magazine down on the cushion beside her and shot past the open French doors, muttering about Brandon's failing eyesight. She returned quickly, apparently convinced that Brandon hadn't somehow missed Serena in Endora's rather large but fenced and gated interior garden. "She's been here all morning."

"Alone?"

"Drew was with her, but he left over a half an hour ago. I walked him to the door myself."

"Why weren't you outside with her?" Brandon clenched his fists, tamping down the urge to grab her and shake her. "You were supposed to be watching her, Samantha!"

"I *was* watching her!" She pushed around him and shot up the winding staircase in the foyer. "She must have just gone to her room the back way or something."

They searched and found nothing. They called the spa on the off chance she might have simply and conveniently forgotten to stay put and had gone in to work. David assured them that neither he nor any other member of the staff, all of whom were present and working, had talked to her all day. Brandon took deep breaths, questioned Miss Lily, who'd been in her kitchen baking while Franklin, her son, repaired the refrigerator right beside her. They'd seen nothing.

Endora also hadn't seen Serena. After talking to Drew, she'd sensed that Serena wanted to be alone. Surprisingly, she'd given her her space, picking a damn fine day to rein in her motherly meddling.

"Calm down, Brandon. She's fine."

"You don't *know* that, Endora."

Sitting behind her ornate, gold and filigree French Renaissance desk in her library, Endora inhaled deeply, closed her eyes and placed her palms flat on the glass top. Her multiple rings and acrylic fingernails tapped the shiny surface. Apparently, she was consulting her psychic sources. Brandon shifted his weight from foot to foot. He didn't buy Endora's mumbo jumbo, but he'd take any lead he could get.

"I know," Endora said just as he was about to turn and leave. "She's unharmed and out of any danger—physically. Emotionally—" her eyes popped open like twin emeralds, flashing with unspoken accusation "—that's another story entirely."

Brandon shrugged off her lucky guess.

"I don't suppose Casper and his friends can tell me where she is?"

Her gaze dropped as she proceeded to tidy the collection of scarves and beads and bottles that littered her desk. "Ask Samantha."

Samantha?

He rushed out and down the stairs, nearly colliding with Serena's sister on the bottom landing.

"I found this in the mailbox." She thrust the quarter-folded sheet of white paper at him. Even before he read the entire threat, his heart stopped. Hot bile surged up the back of his throat and his eyes burned with bound fury.

"'Home is where the heart is...and other body parts.'" He followed the twisted cliché with a string of expletives that made even jaded Samantha flinch.

"Do you want me to call the police?"

Brandon shook his head. Think. Think! He didn't have time to wait for the cops or the patience to turn the investigation over to anyone else. Not yet. *He* was the one who'd promised to protect her. *He* was the one who loved her.

"The stalker wouldn't have left a note for us if he didn't want us to find her. *Home is where the heart is...home is where the heart is*," he repeated.

He conveniently left off the threatening part, knowing that stoking his fear wouldn't help him rationalize. If he acted quickly enough, he would find her, unharmed, all body parts still intact and assembled in the unique and irreplaceable form of Serena Deveaux.

Serena Deveaux, the woman he loved, with everything that was his and him.

Damn it.

"Home...home...*home* is the key word. Whose home?"

"Not this home. We've searched everywhere," Sam assured him.

"Then we have two choices—the stalker's home, or Serena's. He knows where she lives, and he knows we know. That's where he found the original messages to copy, where he tossed that brick to let her know he knew where she lived. I'm outta here."

"I'll come with you!"

"No! Call the police and then follow."

Brandon was out the door and in his Jeep, engine revving and tires peeling, before he realized that when he'd left, Samantha Deveaux had flashed him her best Hollywood smile.

SERENA BUSIED HERSELF cleaning up her living room to the sound of Cajun music on the CD player. Her tiny, old house felt entirely too quiet. Maurice wasn't snoring in the corner. Tabby wasn't meowing for milk in the pantry.

Brandon wasn't watching her every move, teasing her with his magnetic gaze, daring her with his incredible body...torturing her with a future that would never, ever be.

With the exception of her copycat stalker, her plan to reset the direction of her life had completely succeeded. Drew had called off the wedding and didn't hate her for not loving him the way he deserved. She'd had a glorious, unforgettable night of passion with Brandon, the one man she'd always desired and truly loved, thus undoing all the negative karma of the past fifteen years. They couldn't be together for much longer, but she had accepted that from the beginning and she couldn't change the inevitable.

By all accounts, she would soon be marching on with her live-for-the-day, enjoy-the-moment lifestyle. The universe was righted; the forces of negativity and evil would soon be vanquished; simplicity and tranquillity fully restored.

So how come she felt so miserable?

She wandered to the front window and scratched off a leftover smudge of glue from the fresh installation of glass. Scanning the empty street, she saw no sign of either Brandon or Samantha. She thought it completely odd that Brandon would ask her sister to bring her home and then leave her alone, but she trusted he knew what he was doing. He'd ordered new, shatter-proof windows and installed multiple locks on all the doors. Sammie promised to remain somewhere nearby, out of sight, watching her, proving to Brandon what a clever and attentive bodyguard she would make if he'd give her a chance.

For all Serena knew, Brandon had figured out who'd copied her threats and broken her window and was now filing a statement with the police, saving her the red tape. On the other hand, if Brandon didn't know the identity of her stalker yet, she halfway hoped the maniac would come after her, so long as Sammie and Brandon had planned the whole afternoon around catching the crazy and putting him or her behind bars. She didn't mind being bait, though she'd rather she knew about it in advance. But a plan as wildly dangerous as that was definitely up Samantha's movie-magic alley. And with Brandon so desperate to get out of her life, he might just agree to such risky theatrics.

She ran the vacuum for as long as she could stand to, then returned to the pile of dusty board games her sister had left at her house. She pulled out a long black cylinder, uncapped the end and rolled out the leathery lambskin playing board and flattened, colored-glass playing pieces of Pente. She and Brandon had spent hours playing this game after Aunt Tillie bought it for Brandon's twelfth birthday. Tucking her skirt beneath her knees, she sat on the hardwood floor between her living room and kitchen and set up the board, lining the emerald-green stones in the appropriate squares, but cupping the claret-colored set in the palm of her hand.

She toyed with the cool glass, rolling them across her skin, likening the tinkling sound and icy feel to droplets of cold water from her fountain. Determined not to relive that particular memory so soon, she scattered the pieces onto the board and tried to remember how to play the game.

Something about trapping your opponent. She wondered if Brandon remembered the rules or if they could, after he arrived with the good news of her freedom from her stalker, while away the rest of the afternoon in a friendly game.

Trouble was, she and Brandon didn't have the capacity to have a friendly game any more than they could manage a longer-than-one-night affair. For them, competition was endless and cutthroat. Stakes soared and passions ran hotter than the fire in a kiln. From that very first dart game she'd challenged him to just three days ago, to their lovemaking at the spa last night, they'd pushed each other over the brink of reality into the world of extraordinary. They'd each tested and tasted the sweet-spicy flavors of victory, climax and passions most intense.

At least when they made love, nobody lost. Serena had never felt such fulfillment or satisfaction. And she was one hundred percent certain that Brandon hadn't walked away wanting either. Now that the passion was sated, now that she knew how desperately he wanted a future that couldn't include her, the games were truly over. But no matter how the affair ended, neither one of them could claim a long-term prize. If they stayed together much longer, they'd burn each other out. If they parted, her heart would be utterly broken, and she was fairly certain Brandon wouldn't walk away entirely unscathed either. Yet they'd recover as they had before.

Just as she scooped the last of the flat red marbles and slid them into a velvet drawstring pouch, her front door burst open in a shattering hail of splintered wood. Gun drawn, Brandon charged across the foyer, jumping her credenza and scooping her up by the waist. He thrust her behind him and threw her back against the wall. Shielding her with his body, he panted with rage and fear and bravado as he surveyed the empty house with the barrel of his gun.

"Where is he?"

"Where is who? Brandon, what the hell are you doing? I know you didn't like my front lock, but that's no reason to go kicking in my door!"

She tried to sneak around him, but he swung her back against the wainscoting and blocked her path. "Where's the stalker?"

"Didn't I hire you to answer that question?"

Brandon lowered his gun slightly, indicating that he had relaxed, but Serena saw no other evidence, from the pressure he used to hold her against the wall to the glare of anger in his black gaze. "You were gone. We got this note." He grabbed a crumpled sheet of paper from his pocket and thrust it at her. "Weren't you kidnapped by the stalker?"

Serena read the threat, but felt none of the danger the words implied. Not with Brandon pressing so close to her. Not with his gun drawn and his testosterone pumping and his eyes flashing as if they were about to make love. He really was the most magnificent man she'd ever known.

God, she was hopeless!

She swallowed a sigh and refolded the note, shoving it back in his pocket. "Kidnapped? Not unless Samantha is my stalker. She told me you asked her to bring me here. I assumed she was watching from a distance."

Her explanation hung in the air while the dust settled. Her heart, which she suddenly realized was racing, stabilized into a more regular beat. Then, the truth dawned like a brilliant sun over an eastern bayou— slightly hard on the eyes, but impossible to miss.

"Samantha?" he asked, holstering his weapon and dropping his shoulders along with his jaw. "Samantha is your stalker?"

Serena stopped to think. It all made absolute sense— especially because Samantha was a Deveaux and subscribed to a different form of logic than the average person. "Of course she is. How could I have missed it? That little minx!"

"Minx? She threatened your life, Serena. Maybe your sister harbors some serious resentment because you stayed in New Orleans with your mother and she was shipped off to L.A. with dear old brilliant, but broke, Dad."

Serena leveled him with a look of impatience. "Brandon, you know my mother. What kind of resentment could Samantha possibly feel for not having grown up in Endora's shadow? For goodness' sake, Daddy wasn't always broke. He gave her the world and the Hollywood sign to boot. That isn't what this is about."

Serena pushed Brandon aside, which was surprisingly easy now that he'd been officially stunned to silence by the infamous Deveaux way of thinking. She marched past the scattered Pente board and stood in front of what was left of her door, now lying half on the floor and half against her portrait of Miss Lily's favorite cousin, Sarah Blythe.

"I guess I'll have to replace the lock *now*."

She bent to pick up the door and lean it against the shattered frame, but Brandon came up behind her and did the job himself. When the phone rang, Serena stalked away with a frustrated sigh and picked up the portable.

"You owe me one front door, Sammie," Serena said, knowing even without her mother's psychic powers who was on the other end of the line.

"He kicked in the door? Cool! That must have been a sight to see. It looks easy in the movies, but it's really hard on the knees."

Brandon stopped his handiwork to watch her talk, but she marched across the room for a private conversation. "Is this the part in the movie where the villain explains the details of her plan and then leaves the hero and heroine to meet their fate?"

Samantha chuckled on the other end of the line. "I always knew you were more clever than people gave you credit for. You know what I did and why I did it, though you'll probably have to explain it to Brandon. He's fairly bright, but he *is* a man, and by nature they're damn stupid about these things."

Serena turned her back to Brandon, sure that if he saw her concurring smile, he'd think she and Samantha had planned this ruse together from the start.

"One question," Serena posed.

Sammie laughed. "This is so like a B movie. I love it. There's always the one question. Shoot."

"You obviously pilfered Mother's key to the house without telling me, but why were you looking through my casket? All I keep in there are random pieces of paper, most of which I eventually throw out." She bent to retrieve a green Pente stone that had shot across the room in the melee. "Of course, I'm assuming you found the notes by accident and then figured out what I was up to with the fake threats on my life."

"As Mother would say, there are no accidents, only twists of fate. Remember that sweater you bought me for my birthday?"

"The purple one with the feathers on the neckline? It looked fabulous on you!"

"Yeah, well, feathers are your fashion accessory, not mine. But I knew you loved it and the store wouldn't take it back without a receipt..."

Serena laughed until she felt Brandon's presence behind her, hovering, heating her with a warmth that was a potent mixture of frustration, anger, relief and desire.

All vestiges of laughter retreated. Her sister's plan had worked, but not in a way either of them intended. Brandon would be fit to be tied when he heard what Sammie had done. And what Serena was about to do.

"Uh, Samantha...I have to go."

Her sister's chuckle echoed in her ear. "If you get a chance, remind Brandon that I must be incredibly elusive to fool him. Elusive and creative. Maybe even creative enough for him to hire for his firm, license or not."

Brandon slid his palms beneath Serena's elbows and turned her around. His gray eyes smoldered as the rage slowly dissipated and another emotion—raw but volatile—twisted his face. The lines of his jaw were tight, but his hands cupped her with a loving softness that spurred Serena to disconnect the call without saying goodbye.

He took the phone from her and set it down.

"Sam did this to force us together," he said, apparently more practiced in traversing the maze of Deveaux logic than she'd first thought.

"She drove me to your office the other day, and between that conversation and finding the false threats when she was searching for a receipt, she put two and two together. I guess when it looked like I was going to come clean and you would leave, she took over."

"To keep us together."

Serena nodded, and swallowed. God, how she wished her sister could do something now...something dramatic and bold and magical that would somehow waylay the inevitable parting she and Brandon now had to face. Unable to match the intensity of his gaze any longer, she slipped away from him and pretended to inspect the precarious position of her door, propped into the frame and held in place by the antique secretary he'd slid away from the side wall.

"She's very inventive, your sister."

Serena nodded in agreement. Now wasn't the time to talk about Samantha. Now was the time to say goodbye. The mystery was solved. The game was over. She couldn't, wouldn't, bear another minute in his life if she couldn't have forever.

"Looks like you can't use the front door to leave."

"Maybe I don't want to leave."

The words played on her shattering heart; with a hot shiver, she felt the walls and crevices vibrate, as if they would soon meld back into place. But the foundation was tentative—and wouldn't last. She turned to retreat, but he blocked her path, taking her hands in his.

"I've been on some of the most dangerous covert missions ever concocted by the United States Army, and you know what? Until today, until I thought that someone might have taken you from me, I never really knew the taste of fear."

His fingers massaged hers and the fiery friction made her want to kiss him long and deeply, to learn the taste he spoke of, to brand the essence of him into her own senses. But kissing him would only prolong the inevitable. It was time to move on.

"I'm fine, Brandon." She flipped her hands around and took control of his ministrations, stopping his touch before she lost her mind. And body. And soul. "I'll be fine," she assured him—and her—again. "The danger's over. We're over. I'm safe now. You're free to go."

He held her hands tighter. "We'll never be over, Serena. Didn't these fifteen years...didn't last night... teach you anything? I want you in my life."

She shook her hands free and marched away, determined to put some distance between them. Faulty or haphazard though her logic might sometimes be, she knew she was right this time. "Maybe it's not about what you want." Perching her knuckles on her hips, she faced him and reconsidered her argument. "No. That's not right. It's all about what you want. I can't be the woman of your fantasies, Brandon. I can't be your anchor, your ball and chain. That's not who I am. But I also know you deserve that future, if that's what you need to be happy. Warm with a fire in your big stone hearth, dog on your lap, wifey baking barefoot in the kitchen."

She gestured wildly toward her own barely used cooking area and tried to remember the last time she'd even lit her stove without Miss Lily or her mother constructing the meal that was cooked there. She'd made her choices along a different path and she wasn't about to start regretting them now.

Since Brandon kissed her fifteen years ago, she'd rarely allowed herself to truly fantasize about her future beyond the next few days...the next few moments. She'd never planned to be anyone's wife, much less anyone's mother. Over the past few days, she'd learned she wasn't as averse to the idea as she had once been, but that didn't change the fact that her vision of marriage and Brandon's were as different as night and day.

Beyond wanting Brandon—a man she honestly thought she'd never have—three days ago, she would have said her plans for the future were to have a life free from hurt and heartbreak. No life mate. No complications. Friends, family, a prosperous business. An occasional trip to somewhere exciting. An affair now and then to remind her she was a woman.

Simplicity, simplicity, simplicity.

Yet here she was, pushing away the keeper of the other part of her soul. There was nothing simple about this, nothing at all.

Brandon's lips tilted into a grin—half-wistful, half-condescending. "I had a real cute fantasy, didn't I? Naive, definitely. Sort of goofy, if you really think about it."

"Goofy? Not to you. You never had that kind of stability in your childhood. And I certainly can't give it to you now." She looked around her eclectically decorated home, at her outlandish clothes, lifting her arms that jingled from the length of bracelets she wore. "I wish I could."

"No, you don't. At least, I don't." He stopped, instantly realizing that his words stuck in her heart like a thousand hot stickpins. "That's not what I mean."

Grabbing her by the waist, he swung himself onto the couch, then pulled her onto his lap and secured her in a tight grip. "Just sit still and let me explain."

"You don't need to—"

He cut her off by kissing her. Hard. With every inch of his mouth. With every curve of his tongue. No matter how she knew she should pull away, she couldn't. One last taste, she told herself. One last ride on a wave of torrential sensation.

Yet before the pleasure crested, he pulled back, panting with more ferocity than when he'd busted through her door.

"You think I created that fantasy with the wife and kids and two point three dogs because of what I lacked in my childhood. Don't try your hand at conventional rationalization, Serena. It's not your forte."

She knew she should probably be offended, but with his hands stroking her arms and back with rhythmic heat, she could do nothing but listen to his explanation.

"I loved my childhood. I thrived on unpredictability and risk and chance...until my stupid risks tore us apart. So I created this picture after I enlisted that couldn't include you. Made it pretty safe for my ego, constructing a future that I knew damn well you wouldn't want to be a part of."

"What are talking about?"

"I'm talking about the means by which men and women build walls and shape paths to keep the hurt out. Even after last night, even after we shared each other in ways I never imagined, I still couldn't allow myself to dream that we'd find a way to make a future work. How could I? If you denied me, I'd have a part of me missing again. The part that's yours. Is yours. Has always been and will always be...yours."

He slid her right hand over his heart, urging her to measure the rapid pounding as a gauge of his love. She shook her head.

"So I make your heart pound. I turn you on. You do the same to me. But you can't build a future on that."

"Why not?"

"Because..." She paused, not knowing the answer. Conventional wisdom subscribed to the theory that a lasting marriage didn't have good sex as its basis. It was about friendship, trust, honesty. Three things she and Brandon now had together, in addition to the great sex.

"Well?" he pressed.

She huffed. Brandon was offering her everything she wanted. Why couldn't she just accept that?

"Sex isn't enough, Brandon."

His eyes lit with a flame that stopped her protest dead before she could elaborate.

"Wanna bet?"

13

"WHAT ARE YOU talking about?"

She didn't know what he was implying, but she saw the very instant his Chance charm kicked in. Brandon's grin spread so wide across his lushly male, recently kissed mouth that Serena thought his whole gorgeous face might split in two. She didn't know whether to be excited or very, very scared.

"I'm talking about the language we both understand best."

"Sex?"

When she said the word, his eyes darkened. His body grew hard and hot beneath her thigh. Trapped in his arms, she fought the instinct to squirm in his lap or she'd further kindle a flame best kept unlit. They'd already proven their compatibility in the sex department. Never in her entire life had she felt so uninhibited, so wanton and brazen and one with the universe, than she had with Brandon in her erotic garden. But even then, she hadn't considered, hadn't even entertained, what would happen beyond the next morning, beyond the next moment. Hoping would only break her heart.

And yet, she realized now, she couldn't help herself, no matter how irrational and naive hoping for a future with Brandon was.

"Serena, do you remember last night? The way you

opened yourself to me?" He slid one hand over the crevice between her knees, then up to her thighs, using his hands to illustrate his point—an unnecessary action if ever there was one. "The friction of my skin against yours? The pressure of me inside you?"

She willed herself not to blush, but damn it if a prickly heat didn't spread from her belly to her cheeks, then lower, initiating a gentle throbbing of moistening flesh that could be her undoing. "That's not enough to build a relationship on."

"Maybe it isn't...maybe it is. But I don't think that's all we have together. And you don't either."

Her mouth dried. Her heart thudded against her rib cage, so hard she wondered if he could see her quake. She slid her hand between her breasts and willed herself to calm down, then suddenly realized that touching herself in such close proximity to Brandon only tightened her nipples with a hungry ache.

"I don't like where this is leading."

Brandon knew the moment she'd become aroused the same way he knew that he'd have to pull out all the stops to lure her to his way of thinking. Some notions, some phenomena, like the two of them together—forever and for keeps—were too far-fetched for even her to believe. But he wasn't going to let her scoff and dismiss the possibility just because he'd told her his stupid fantasy—meant specifically to keep her out of his future, something he now knew was impossible.

He held her steady, stroked her slowly, teaching her with hands and gaze and hold that he had no intention of releasing her so she could run or hide or pretend the way she had for her entire adult life.

Living for the moment and in the moment had

served her well in the past—but they'd buried the past. Now it was time to fly into an uncertain future. The topsy-turvy sensation of the vast emotional unknown made him thankful he held her tight. Her eyes betrayed her intention to push out of his arms at the first opportunity and run, run, run.

"Not so full of bravado when faced with hard reality, are you?" he asked.

"What hard reality?"

"That you and I are great together."

"In a physical sense."

His face lost all its laughter, his body all its casual mirth. He turned her slightly so she couldn't help but look him straight in the eyes. She could see straight into his soul if only she dared to.

She struggled. He pulled her closer. Nearly nose to nose, she inhaled. He grinned. He wanted her to smell the musky, natural scent of him, mixed with the aroma of torn wood, dust and fear. Fear of her coming to harm. Fear of him losing her forever.

"You don't really think that's all we have, do you? I love you, Serena."

She shook her head, closing her eyes to offset the wild dizziness swirling around her. "I love you, too. I always have. But that doesn't mean..."

The moment he released her, she rolled off the couch to dash...where? Lord, her house was small! No matter where she went, he'd follow. No matter what she said, he'd persist. From the moment she walked into his office—no, even before then—from the instant she heard he was coming back to New Orleans, back into her life, she'd set a course of events in motion that now she couldn't stop.

She stood immobilized in the center of the living room, quivering when she heard the creak of the couch, the soft shuffle of his feet across the rug. He stopped just in front of her, touched her chin with one finger, tilting her face just enough so she could once again witness the depth of his veracity.

"What do you want, Serena?"

Right now, she wanted him to leave. No, that was a lie. She didn't want him to leave. But she didn't want to have this conversation, didn't want to delve into the chamber of her heart where she'd long ago stored away her love for him—a chamber he'd broken into without even trying, a chamber that now leaked pure desire into every aspect of her body and soul.

"I don't understand," she whispered, shaking her head, wondering how he could unravel her with one single touch, wondering how she'd kept herself in one piece so long without him to hold her together.

With his finger, he drew a soft line from chin to cheek, then curled a strand of hair behind her ear in a sweet, guileless gesture. "I told you what I wanted from my future. And today, I realized that the fantasy I'd created was just a way to keep me from loving you. That plan crashed and burned, *chère*. I know now that I want you, need you, have always wanted and needed you. But what do *you* want?"

She couldn't lie to him. Not again. Not anymore. She didn't have the strength. Perhaps the truth would send him packing just as it almost had two nights before.

"I've only ever wanted one thing, Brandon. You. But for so long, I accepted that we'd never happen—not for the long haul. How could a friendship that ended so easily and an affair that came out of the blue—how could that last? I don't usually think about my life beyond tomorrow, but I can't live that way anymore. I can't lose you again. I can't."

"You won't."

"You don't know that."

"I'll prove it."

"How?"

"Marry me."

"What?"

He dipped onto one knee and stole her hand, cradling her palm in his. "Serena Jeanne Deveaux, be my wife. Be my partner. My life mate. My instigator. My rival. My navigator. My heart."

He shifted closer, grabbing her other hand and pressing them both to his lips. "Be my soul. It'll be a crazy ride, but we're both daredevils. We'll survive."

"I don't want to be a daredevil in marriage."

"Serena, that's all either of us knows. Marriage is a risk, the ultimate risk. But we can't back down. I love you. You love me. We don't have a choice."

"Life is all about choice."

"And about challenges."

"Brandon..."

"That's it!"

To hell with the traditional bended-knee and sappy pour-out-your-heart crap. Brandon stood and lifted Serena in one movement, beating down the impulse to haul her over his shoulder, and cradling her against his chest instead. Serena Deveaux had always operated on a different plane than the rest of the world, but it was time she faced regular old three-dimensional reality—Chance style.

"What are you doing?"

Her voice rose with protest, but she didn't struggle nearly enough to convince him to put her down, which he ultimately did, once they'd reached her bedroom and he'd kicked the door shut behind him.

"You want me to work for this, don't you? I'm game, Serena. I'm always game. There are two languages you and I understand. One is sex. Duly noted. The other is challenge. So here it is."

He rolled with her onto the bed, pinning her beneath him. She was as soft as her purple satin comforter, but the slick material was cool compared to the heated temperature of her skin. He captured her wrists, held them next to her ears and issued his proposal again— this time in words he knew she couldn't resist.

"I dare you."

"You *dare* me? To what? Sleep with you? I did that."

"Technically, no, you didn't. We made love, we had sex," he amended. "But we didn't wake up in each other's arms, not like married people do, knowing that morning isn't the end, but just another beginning. We wanted each other for the moment. This time it will be different. I love you. I know you love me. I dare you to spend the next twenty-four hours with me, in this room, in this bed. If you decide you want to walk away from me tomorrow, you're free to go. If you still think I could ever walk away, I'll do just that. I'll even up the ante. I'll leave New Orleans."

"No!"

"Then you accept my challenge?"

"Brandon, this is ridiculous."

Dragging her arms over her head, he captured her wrists in one hand, then shifted his weight so he could run the other across her forehead, down her cheek, along her throat. He slid his fingers between her breasts, then skimmed the curves beneath them, watching her nipples pucker through the snug cotton of her sleeveless blouse.

"I double-dare you." He whispered the words against the base of her throat, sliding his palm downward, deviating only to warm the bare flesh of her belly at the hem of her shirt. He felt her tremble. He heard her sigh.

"Brandon, this isn't the time for games and bets," she said, but the sweet sound of resignation urged him on. She knew he would win, but that didn't make the challenge any less invigorating. She was Serena, after all.

"This is the perfect time for games, sweetheart." He dragged his hand over the filmy cotton of her sarong skirt, first where it hugged her hip, then to the slit that had invariably fallen open to invite his hot touch against her sweet, bare thigh. "Am I going to have to triple-dog-dare you or is there another way I can ensure your agreement?"

The sensations of his touch blinded her. The power of his words set her heart aflame. How could she deny this man? How could she deny her heart? She loved him. She wanted him. In her body. In her life. For all time. As his wife.

Yes! Complications be damned. If life were meant to be simple, the masters of the universe wouldn't have brought her and Brandon together.

Fate couldn't be denied. Love couldn't be ignored.

But she didn't have to tell him that—yet. Not with a challenge on the table.

She tugged her wrists free with ease since his concentration seemed to center on untying the knot on her skirt rather than holding her still. With a single push, she rolled him over and straddled his waist, just as the knot unraveled and her skirt fell aside to reveal nothing underneath but soft curls and bare skin. In a flash of pure wantonness, she ripped her tank top over her head and threw it aside. She was atop him, naked and fired and free.

And not yet ready to tip her hand.

"What are your terms again?" she asked, folding her arms across her chest.

Brandon groaned when her pose enhanced the size and shape of her breasts. She was trying to distract him again. And she was seriously succeeding. After taking a moment to caress her with his gaze, he folded his hands behind his head and smiled as if he was merely holding a royal flush over his lap instead of a glorious, naked woman.

A naked woman who loved him.

"The simplest terms we've ever dealt with. We make love. We talk. We eat. We make love. We pull out that Pente game I nearly tripped over, ice up those marbles, draw a grid on your belly and see where it leads."

He started unbuttoning his shirt, but she slapped his hands aside and worked the buttons herself.

"So we bet our whole future on a game of Pente?"

"We bet our future on the morning. If you aren't the most satisfied, most deliriously happy woman that ever existed in New Orleans or beyond, I leave, no questions asked."

He leaned forward, shed his shirt, wrapped his arms around her waist and buried his face in the curve between her breasts. He inhaled deeply, then blew a cool directed breath across the tips of her breasts, licked them, then blew again.

Serena arched her back and closed her eyes while sensations wild and wicked stole through her. He kissed her, caressed her, stroked, teased and pinched until all her fears unraveled into gossamer threads of desire. She sighed and concentrated, willing herself to form at least one more coherent thought before she completely and totally surrendered to the magic he wove.

"And if I am the most satisfied, most deliriously happy woman in New Orleans and beyond in the morning? What do I lose?"

He chuckled as he rolled her back beneath him, shed his jeans and briefs, grabbed her by the knees and slid her down the slick surface of her bedspread so her legs dangled over the side.

"All your inhibitions?" he offered, tugging on the edges of the Mardi Gras boa collection she kept wrapped around her bedposts. He tossed the emerald and gold ones aside, lifted her leg and tied the thin, purple downy one around her ankle.

While he fastened the other end to the footboard, she drew her toes across his midsection and teased the tip of his straining sex. "I don't have any inhibitions." She grabbed the discarded emerald boa and cast the strand of feathers over his shoulder like a fishing line. "Not with you. What else can I lose?"

He secured her legs, then bent over her, tasted her lips, her earlobes, her throat while he stole the golden boa from her grasp and teased her nipples with the glittered tips of the feathers.

"What about your heart?"

"It's already yours, Brandon."

"Then I have nothing left to win and you have nothing to lose."

"Seems like a win-win situation to me. Why even bother with the game?"

"Oh, I don't know. A dare is a dare and a bet is a bet. You wouldn't want a man who'd welsh on a wager, would you?"

She would have said no if she'd still controlled her power to speak. But when his mouth and body drifted downward, loving her inch by slow inch, she could only moan and sigh and surrender, knowing that this one time forfeiting her soul would produce the most glorious win of all.

Epilogue

SERENA AND BRANDON awoke to a cacophony of thunder, lightning and charging rain. The darkness of the storm extended the night into morning. Good loving stretched the morning into the afternoon...then to the evening. By seven o'clock, Serena finally left her bed. She'd admitted "defeat" in Brandon's sensual game hours ago, but as the most satisfied woman in New Orleans, she didn't care about losing one bit.

Her sister borrowed Endora's key one last time and on the kitchen table left a Crock-Pot full of jambalaya, the name and number of a good carpenter and a manila envelope filled with travel brochures perfect for a honeymoon.

After scoring two spoons and a bottle of wine, Serena hefted the jambalaya back into the bedroom where she and Brandon ate, kissed, drank, touched and planned a few months into the future.

"I've always wanted to go to Tahiti," Serena mused before Brandon shoveled a spoonful of spicy rice-and-meat mixture into her mouth. She chewed a morsel of shrimp, inhaling at the heat of the cayenne Miss Lily used with a generous hand.

Brandon slipped the brochure from her fingers and stacked it in the "yes" pile atop Casa de Campo, Rio de Janeiro and Monaco. He'd claimed to enjoy the traveling most of all during his tour in the army—and Serena was quite certain she'd make a hell of a better bunk mate.

"That's four places," he counted. "One week in each and a little in between for travel. Should we charter our own plane or do it like real tourists?"

"Looks like we're heading for the full tourist treatment, complete with the debt."

Brandon grinned and took two more ravenous bites. "Don't worry about debt. My parents weren't the only ones to make a little mad money at the roulette tables. I sunk a chunk into the business, but I didn't buy more than the essentials, so I have cash to spare."

"And you do have my fifteen hundred dollars," she reminded him, slithering across the well-rumpled and well-warmed sheets to retrieve the nearly empty bottle of Beaujolais they'd been sipping like soda with dinner. She took a swig and then handed the rest to him.

"True," he concluded, grinning slyly at his own lack of remorse for taking her money. Well, he *had* saved her. From herself. From her silly notion that they weren't absolutely meant for each other. That was worth at least a couple of thousand.

He chugged down the last of the wine and sorted through another colorful trifold advertisement. "Let's add Aspen, too. We can recover from sunburn on the icy slopes."

She shook her head as he tossed yet another brochure to the growing pile, the remnants of her purple boa dangling from his wrist. She anticipated replacing the feathery string at Carnival next year, and the thrill of experiencing all that was New Orleans with Brandon imbued her with an excitement she hadn't felt in years. This was the way things should have been. And now they were.

So simple.

"I can't leave the spa this long, Brandon. And you just started your business."

He moved the Crock-Pot from the center of the bed to the floor, palmed the winning brochures aside with all the skill of a card shark and scooted the rest away in a flutter. In an instant, she was pinned beneath him, naked and full from good food and wine, yet hungry and thirsty for him and him alone.

"We'll get married just before summer break and David can run the spa while you're gone. As for No Chances Protection, I figure Samantha has earned her shot."

"Really?"

She encircled his neck with her arms and pulled herself up to peck him on the cheek. If Brandon was willing to take a chance on her sister after the stunt she'd pulled, she owed him a lot more than just a kiss. Actually, they both owed Sammie a great deal. Giving her a new job seemed the least they could do. As soon as they returned from their honeymoon, Serena was going to find her sister a man of her own. She simply didn't know what she was missing.

"Thank you, Brandon. Sammie will do a great job, you'll see."

He groaned his halfhearted agreement, but made it clear with exploring hands and lips that he wanted a lot more than an innocent kiss for his trouble. She decided a sweeter price had never been paid.

He claimed her mouth greedily, touching her, arousing her, until she was dizzy with need and begging

him to slip inside and turn her world from thunder-
storm gray to orgasmic white.

And just like a Chance man, he rose to the challenge.

* * * * *

Look for Samantha's story this June!

Pamela Burford presents

The Wedding Ring

Four high school friends and a pact—
every girl gets her ideal mate by thirty or be
prepared for matchmaking! The rules are
simple. Give your "chosen" man three
months...and see what happens!

Love's Funny That Way
Temptation #812—on sale December 2000
It's no joke when Raven Muldoon falls in love with comedy
club owner Hunter—*brother* of her "intended."

I Do, But Here's the Catch
Temptation #816—on sale January 2001
Charli Ross is more than willing to give up her status as
last of a dying breed—the thirty-year-old virgin—to Grant.
But all *he* wants is marriage.

One Eager Bride To Go
Temptation #820—on sale February 2001
Sunny Bleecker is still waiting tables at Wafflemania when
Kirk comes home from California and wants to marry her.
It's as if all her dreams have finally come true—except...

Fiancé for Hire
Temptation #824—on sale March 2001
No way is Amanda Coppersmith going to let
The Wedding Ring rope her into marriage. But no matter
how clever she is, Nick is one step ahead of her...

"Pamela Burford creates the
memorable characters readers love!"
—*The Literary Times*

It's hot...and it's out of control.

BLAZE

This winter is going to be hot, hot, hot!
Don't miss these bold, provocative,
ultra-sexy books!

SEDUCED by Janelle Denison
December 2000

Lawyer Ryan Matthews wanted sexy Jessica Newman the moment he saw her. And she seemed to want him, too, but something was holding her back. So Ryan decides it's time to launch a sensual assault. He *is* going to have Jessica in his bed—and he isn't above tempting her with her own forbidden fantasies to do it....

SIMPLY SENSUAL by Carly Phillips
January 2001

When P.I. Ben Callahan agrees to take the job of watching over spoiled heiress Grace Montgomery, he figures it's easy money. That is, until he discovers gorgeous Grace has a reckless streak a mile wide and is a serious threat to his libido—and his heart. Ben isn't worried about keeping Grace safe. But can he protect her from his loving lies?

Don't miss this daring duo!

Tyler Brides

It happened one weekend...

Quinn and Molly Spencer are delighted to accept three
bookings for their newly opened B&B, Breakfast Inn Bed,
located in America's favorite hometown, Tyler, Wisconsin.

But Gina Santori is anything but thrilled to discover her
best friend has tricked her into sharing a room with
the man who broke her heart eight years ago....

And Delia Mayhew can hardly believe that she's
gotten herself locked in the Breakfast Inn Bed
basement with the sexiest man in America.

Then there's Rebecca Salter. She's turned up at the
Inn in her wedding gown. Minus her groom.

*Come home to Tyler for three delightful novellas
by three of your favorite authors: Kristine Rolofson,
Heather MacAllister and Jacqueline Diamond.*

HARLEQUIN®
Makes any time special ™